ON FRAGILE WAVES

E. Lily Yu

EREWHON

This is a work of fiction. All of the characters, organizations, and events portrayed in this novel are either products of the author's imagination or are used fictitiously.

ON FRAGILE WAVES
Copyright © 2021 by E. Lily Yu

Edited by Liz Gorinsky

Erewhon Books
2 W. 29th Street, Suite 3S
New York, NY 10001
www.erewhonbooks.com

Erewhon books are available at special discounts when purchased in bulk for premiums and sales promotions as well as for fundraising or educational use. Special editions or book excerpts can also be created to specification. For details, send an email to specialmarkets@workman.com.

Library of Congress Control Number: 2020950745

ISBN 978-1-64566-009-5 (hardcover)
ISBN 978-1-64566-012-5 (ebook)

Cover design by Kimberly Glyder
Cover and interior kelp image by kjohansen / istockphoto
Cover pearl image by Exlusively / Shutterstock
Ornamental image of waves by Laymik from the Noun Project

Printed in the United States of America

First Edition: February 2021
10 9 8 7 6 5 4 3 2 1

For those who have lost

ON
FRAGILE
WAVES

PART
ONE

CHAPTER ONE

Once there was ⎫
Once there wasn't ⎬ a daughter

   tak

           daz daz daz daz daz
      grumb   *bamp*
  shrak   born during

                         tak

      damb   *tas tas tas tas tas*

                             war

when time is no time at all and everything must be said in the
breath between
    mortar————————————————————fire

We will call her Firuzeh her father said
slapping her back until she purpled and wailed
because she will either be a rock or victorious
and besides, a name is cheaper than a sword

Her first word was *gola*

I ask you, what is the difference between war and not-war
when there is no music

Two years later came Nour
slick and shiny
in a long unsatisfied scream
and everyone was hungrier.

When Firuzeh was six, fire fell again from the sky

ghrumb   *ghrumb*   *ghrumb*

A city of smoke pitched its tents over Kabul. A long loud time.
Amrika on every lip.

Then Abay turned on the radio
and on the fragile waves they heard
a dambura strumming a milk-and-sugar song.
It's over, thank God, said Atay, and went to work.

CHAPTER TWO

Listen said Abay bring me your clothes to pack and I will tell you the story of Rostam and Rakhsh.

At least sit still, Nour, and don't tear down the laundry
At least sit
Nour—please—
Rostam was rash and brave like you, light of my eyes, and when the time came to find him a steed, every horse buckled under his warrior's weight.

So they ran the best horses of Kabul past him, the swiftest and most beautiful, and just like your Atay feels the engine of a Corolla throbbing through the hood and knows how well it runs, you could feel the proud heartbeat of these horses.

God knows stabling horses wasn't a dangerous job then;
no one threatened the Kabuli stable keepers who paraded their horses for this prince.

We should have stayed servants—but your father is proud.
Anyhow—

Rostam cut from the herd a beautiful colt spotted like rose petals on saffron,

like the silk flowers from Chicken Street on a wedding taxi.

He tossed his lasso around its neck and asked the price of the horse.

If you are Rostam, said the herdsman, its price is nothing less than this country—go forth and defend it.

So Rostam and Rakhsh traveled forth seeking adventure

as we are all about to do

and Rakhsh kept Rostam safe, as your Atay and I will keep you safe.

Rakhsh guarded Rostam while he slept. First he killed a lion that crept up in the night. In the morning Rostam discovered shreds of lion in his horse's teeth and on his horse's hooves.

Then Rakhsh kicked Rostam awake when a dragon approached.

Once.

Twice.

Both times Rostam saw nothing. He threatened to kill the useless son of a donkey if he was woken up again.

The third time, Rostam saw the dragon and slew it, and praised Rakhsh—how he praised him, light of my eyes.

Deeply did Rostam love Rakhsh, as much as a mother loves her son.

They rode together for many years and countless farsang, until treachery—

but that is another story.

We will ride a bus to Jalalabad tonight, just as Rostam rode Rakhsh to challenge the White Div. In Jalalabad we will change buses the way Persian warriors changed horses and ride to Pakistan. It will be like a story.

I need you to be good

I need you to be quiet

I need you to not pull Firuzeh's hair, Nour

I pass our Quran over you, so you are blessed. Kiss it. Now you. No, it will stay here, to protect our home while we are gone.

Put on your shoes.

CHAPTER THREE

The ripped vinyl of the seat caught Firuzeh's skirt as she shifted to peek out of the minibus window. Nour's elbow dug into her side.

Atay, are we in Pakistan yet?

Not yet, Nour.

How much longer?

A little while.

You said that when we were on the bus.

It's still true. Don't kick.

You liked the plush German bus, didn't you? And the trucks that bumped up and down but had beautiful eyes on their back gates and flowers and lions on their sides?

Yes, Abay.

I didn't. They hurt my bum. Firuzeh has more bum, that's why hers doesn't hurt.

I liked the sheep on the truck. It was soft.

This one's too crowded. Everyone smells.

You smell, Nour.

Just a little longer, Nour jan. A few more minutes and we'll be at the border.

Will there be police, Atay?

Enough. I need to remember four hundred things today. Ask your mother.

Will the police stop us, Abay?

What a question.

Are we going to get in trouble?

Do you want to know something? For a few afghanis you can cross the border into Pakistan unhindered. That is how day workers flow in and out with a little more money in their pockets. The tide of adventurers—that's what we are—flows in and does not return. It is not dangerous at all, Firuzeh, not like what Bibinegar had to do.

What did Bibinegar have to do?

She had to win back her husband Khastehkhomar from a demoness and stay alive.

And did she?

If you're going to tell stories in front of everyone—Atay rubbed his eyes—at least do it properly. From the beginning. The snake.

All right. One day among days a woodcutter found a snake in his bundle, thick as your Atay's arm. He almost died of fear right there, but the snake said, I will not harm you if you marry me to your daughter. Bibinegar was a brave girl and agreed. On their wedding night, when the guests were gone, the snake flung off his skin and became a beautiful young man, Khastehkhomar. And they lived very happily together.

But the women had to gossip and say idle, foolish things. Atay sighed. Isn't that always so?

Abay said: If Firuzeh married a snake who was also a man, wouldn't you try to make him less snake and more man?

If that snake tried his nonsense with *my* daughter, I'd have beaten him to death.

Or taken her and fled the country.

Abay, is that why we had to leave?

Listen to the story, Nour.

Firuzeh eats too much and won't let me win at walnuts— who'd want her?

Why not ask him how to destroy his skin, Bibinegar's mother said. To make him stay. So Bibinegar asked Khastehkhomar, and he said, if you must know, you can burn it in a fire of onion skins and garlic peels. But if you do that, I will leave you forever. And Bibinegar told her mother all this.

That old woman probably wept, wrung her hands, tore her hair, said shame! and all those things that mothers-in-law do. Of course that silly girl bent under all that pressure. Of course the skin was burned.

Did you want to tell this story, husband?

Please, go on.

Khastehkhomar smelled the smoke from afar and knew what had happened. He came to his wife and said, so you've done it. Now I must leave you. She wept and said, Is there no other way? And Khastehkhomar said, Only if you walk until you wear out seven pairs of iron shoes to reach Mount Qaf, where my relatives the peris live, which is where I am going. So Bibinegar—

Enough. They're asleep.

No . . . I'm—not . . .

You say this man is trustworthy?

As trustworthy as any of them. He's gotten six men to Australia.

Where's Australia?

I don't know. But it's safe, he said. The children will go to good schools. No one will attack me in the street, or leave threatening letters, or insult you.

The right question to ask a smuggler like that, one of the other passengers interjected, is—how many men did he fail to get to Australia?

I did not ask him that.

Then God help you.

You speak from experience?

I had a Herati cousin headed to Germany through Iran. Haven't heard from him in months. They found some boys dead in a cargo container, but he wasn't among them. The smuggler has left Herat, for who-knows-where. And you, you have a wife and children—

Quiet, please. Don't wake them. They don't need to be frightened.

How else do children learn?

Firuzeh cracked her eyes open. In front of her, wedged among tightly corded bundles, a chukar swayed in its wire cage, staring, its black pupil ringed in brown then red. Destined for battle. To claw and draw blood and finally be eaten. Now and then a jolt of the minibus knocked a querulous note from its throat.

And she, and she—

Was Rostam on his speckled steed, riding into unknown lands.

Was Bibinegar in iron shoes, gone to Mount Qaf, where wonders were.

Was as disobedient as snake-shouldered Zahhak when she pinched her brother and made him wail, or so Abay often said.

Goodbye to Homaira, goodbye to Sheringol, goodbye to the dry, sweet smell of the classroom where she learned her lessons, where the harried teacher always called on someone else, never mind that Firuzeh leaned almost on tiptoe from her desk, vibrating with answers.

Goodbye to home and the creaking, clanging front gate, and the steaming vats of breakfast pulses by the road, and the men sitting in wheelbarrows, waiting for work.

Goodbye to the mountains sharp with snow.

Atay gestured toward a stranger. Agha, do you know how much longer . . .

Only an hour or so to the border. Where are you going?

Peshawar.

Where in Peshawar?

I don't know. I have a name, a phone number—

Fool, the stranger said amiably. A name and a phone number, a name and a phone number, all the way to Australia—is that how you'll go? God protect you.

Abay said: My husband is no fool.

A long, sad look. Then the stranger proffered a pocketful of dried mulberries. For the children, he said, and turned to face the front, and from then until Peshawar he did not speak again.

CHAPTER FOUR

Firuzeh was sleepy and stumbling when they reached the compound in Peshawar. A door opened; lamplight flared. A paper cutout of a man, smelling of garlic and cigarettes, rippled out to greet them.

A pleasure to meet you, a pleasure. I am Abdullah Khan. What are you waiting for? he said to the driver of the dingy car they had come in.

You said two thousand rupees.

Come back for it tomorrow.

But—

Am I not good for my word?

The driver retreated. Abdullah Khan threw his arm around Atay's shoulders. Come in, welcome.

Up the stairs. Three narrow beds in a dark and musty room. On the windowsill, a brown stick clawed upward from its pot.

You'll wait here, Abdullah Khan said. Until we have your documents and tickets ready.

How long? Abay said, her eyes measuring the room.

We don't know. But don't worry, we'll take care of it. He applied a lighter to a cigarette. The rent is modest, one hundred fifty rupees a night.

But we already paid twenty thousand dollars in Kabul—

Hearing a mouse's noise, Firuzeh popped her head out the door. Down the dim hall, a plump-cheeked girl peered out of another doorway.

They regarded each other silently for a moment. The yellow ruffles of the strange girl's dress, the glossy crimp of her hair, and the leather daisy on her shoe smacked of having, owning, ordering. Then the strange girl pulled a face and vanished back into her room.

Firuzeh took two steps down the hall, and then Abdullah Khan was backing out of the door, effusive and firm. His smile did not quite reach his eyes. Even as Atay continued to protest, left hand gesticulating, his right hand descended on Firuzeh's shoulder and steered her back inside.

Behave.

This is Agha Rahmatullah Shahsevani, Khanem Delruba, and Nasima. They're also going to Australia. Firuzeh jan, what do you say?

We were here first, the girl in the yellow dress said, folding her arms.

Hello, Firuzeh mumbled. Then: Why doesn't Nour have to say anything?

Because I'm younger than you, stupid.

I'm sure the girls will get along. No, Nasima is the youngest, we have three altogether. Jawed and Khairullah are in Perth already. Working. We're going to join them.

Do you believe what they say? How long will we have to wait?

They're honest men. They got our sons to Perth.

Where did you work, Agha Rahmatullah?

In the government.

My father is very important, Nasima said, fidgeting with the cloth of her skirt. People ask him for permissions, stamps, and signatures. Is your father important?

He's like the stable keeper who brought Rakhsh to Rostam, Firuzeh said.

He fixes automobiles, Nour said. Ow! Firuzeh!

Are they charging us too much for our rooms? What's the rate for a room in Peshawar?

God knows, Delruba said.

We've paid fortunes already, Rahmatullah said. This is a trifle. A sneeze.

We don't have any sneezes left.

Is your family poor? Nasima said. You don't look like you have much money.

Look at them, friends already. Such sweet kids.

I like your shoes, Firuzeh said, angry and shy and confused.

Thank you. They are real leather. Made in Iran. And yours are—?

The boys couldn't keep their mouths shut, Rahmatullah said. If there was a petition, they signed it. If there was a movement, they joined it.

The letters we would get! His head and beard went white, see?

It cost us almost everything we had to send them to Australia. Now they send us back a little here, a little there—

They are good boys. If dumb as oxen.

Is your brother dumb too? Nasima said.

Very.

The two girls turned their heads to appraise Nour. He had abandoned their conversation to watch an ant march along the window, through slashes of sunlight, up the flowerpot and across the hardened dirt.

It seems so, Nasima said, nodding sagely. But you and me, we know what's going on.

We do, Firuzeh said, not having the faintest idea.

And when we arrive, my father will find a good job. An important job. My brothers will be kind to me instead of insufferable. And now that they don't need to send their money home, they can buy me kilos and kilos of lollies—that's what sweets are called there. They promised. And my mother will dye my father's hair black again, so you can't tell how much he worried, and I will wear the best clothes and go to the best school—

She took a breath. Her cheeks were flushed, her eyes shining.

What about you?

That's a dream for rich people, Firuzeh said.

Atay often said that when he came home, hands and face black with oil, before swinging Nour, then Firuzeh, around in circles. Someday silk for your mother, ice cream for you, a suit for me, and a palace for all of us—but who am I fooling? That's a dream for—

Well, you're no fun, Nasima said.

CHAPTER FIVE

After nine days, Abdullah Khan returned with deep blue passports and plane tickets, which he doled out like largesse.

You're Hungarian now, he said. A little swagger in his step. A little smirk on his lips. O what a trick, what a trickster, to treat borders like jump ropes.

This flight is to Australia? Atay said.

Ha. If we sent you direct to Australia, you'd be caught and deported at once—no good. You're going to Jakarta. I have a friend there who'll take care of you.

He'll send us to Australia?

Eventually, eventually. You must trust us. We would never let anything happen to those children of yours. Look at those beautiful smiles. Imagine them safe in Australia, writing a letter to Qaqa Abdullah Khan. Thank you so much Uncle for sending us here—

Firuzeh, who had not at any point been smiling, pulled the corners of her mouth downward with her fingers.

When are we leaving? Abay said.

Now. The car's in the courtyard.

Can we say goodbye to that nice family—

No time. Take your things, let's go.

Five minutes later, Abdullah Khan chivvying them along, they had swept everything together, wadding up clothes, cramming scarves and washcloths into bags—zippers pulled tight—a sleeve sticking out, forlorn.

The same scarred driver that had brought them to the compound ten nights ago was waiting in the courtyard, honking at regular intervals. His sour expression had sweetened considerably.

As Atay climbed into the taxi, Abdullah Khan clapped him on the back. Go, hurry up, or you'll miss your plane.

He waved at them as the taxi crunched out through the gates. As they turned into the alley, Firuzeh glanced back, thinking she might see Nasima's inquisitive head hanging out a window. But the courtyard was empty.

As soon as they were buckled into their seats on the plane, two on each side of the aisle, Nour began to kick the seat in front of him, singing, We're flying, flying, flying!

The elderly occupant of said seat swung his head around. Slow down, little donkey, we aren't moving yet!

When the engines finally rumbled to life, Nour yelped and shrank into a ball. Abay took Atay's hand, then Firuzeh's. Her palm was damp and slippery.

Atay beamed. Australia soon, he said.

The cabin shook, the engines thundered, and the brown and green patchwork of past-and-no-longer lives shrank to the breadth of a handkerchief and fluttered away.

Then there was nothing to see but a pure, clear sky.

∿∿∿

The man who met them in Jakarta's airport demanded their phones and forged passports—Atay hesitated, then meekly surrendered them—before rushing them into a car. As he drove, he fished a faded turquoise photo of an ocean liner out of the glove compartment and said, in halting English: Your ship. You get on ship like this.

Atay took the photo and fingered its creases as thoughtfully as the beads of a tasbih. This ship?

One like it. Wait, and you'll see.

Their contact brought them to a house in Jakarta, where a ceiling fan stirred the syrupy air. When brushed against, the walls flaked blue paint and plaster. Closing a door quickly flattened brown geckoes in the jambs. In the mornings and evenings, motorcycles churned down the muddy road in front of the house. Behind the house was the enormous concrete wall of a school. The high roar of children reciting lessons and laughing soaked into the cloth of their lives.

Atay went out one afternoon and came back carrying all the colors of the sunset in his perahan.

Here, he said, cutting pieces from a papaya. Try this.

Firuzeh and Nour pulled apart branches of flossy, vermilion rambutan, sugar apples, creamy yellow scales of jackfruit. Nour scraped an entire mango to its pith with his front teeth without offering to share. Firuzeh, her cheeks full of fruit, did not complain.

Zanam, just a little piece.

This foreign fruit will give us stomachaches, Abay said, pushing aside the cube of papaya that Atay offered. Better to have one good orange from Jalalabad, or a clay shell of grapes from the Istalif road.

I'll have her stomachache for her, Nour said, reaching with sticky fingers for the cube of papaya.

Our own little Mullah Nasruddin, Firuzeh muttered.

Entirely in keeping with the general injustice of the universe, Firuzeh fell violently ill later that night, sweating and whimpering over the toilet, while Atay and Nour suffered no ill effects whatsoever.

I told you, Abay sighed. This family's women always suffer.

CHAPTER SIX

As it had in Peshawar, the summons arrived suddenly at night. A truck's headlights flared through the windows. Someone rapped hard on the door. Take your things, you're going, nownownow.

Our documents? Atay said. Our phones?

Here. Hurry up.

Two other families were already packed into the utility truck. Knees and elbows knocked together as Firuzeh's family settled in.

You! Nasima said, her grin a flash in the dark. Did you miss me?

Nope.

You missed me every day. Admit it, Firuzeh, or I'll pull your hair.

Firuzeh answered with decorous silence.

Found other friends, did you?

Thousands of them.

And forgot about me?

Down to your name. Who are you, again? Then Firuzeh, unable to keep her face straight, dissolved into giggles, and Nasima joined in. Abay hushed them, alarmed.

They drove for what felt like hours, until the grit and stones beneath the wheels softened to sandy loam. They were let out into a forest not far from the sea. A crowd had already gathered there, murmuring in six languages.

The sky was veiled and sequined with a quarter moon for an earring and a dowry of stars. Some of the lowest stars were blotted out by a black hulk that creaked and scraped on the sandbar. Nasima whistled softly, and Firuzeh was jealous for a moment, wishing she, too, had older brothers who could teach her how to whistle and spit.

The man who had met them at the airport gave low and urgent orders.

I don't understand, Atay said.

In you go.

How many of us are you putting on that?

All of you.

Are you crazy?

Relax. We've done this many times before.

Three Indonesians waded into the waist-deep water and began to hand the passengers onto the boat. Firuzeh lost count around forty, when the fishing sloop began to list. Once she, Nour, Abay, and Atay were crammed aboard, the last of many, the boat was riding low enough in the water that a rogue wave might have tipped them over.

The passengers arranged their feet carefully, trying not to kick each other. Etiquette was of the utmost importance with so many people in so limited a space.

Ropes slithered and loosened all around them, and with a slap of water against wood, the boat drifted free.

The driver and smuggler watched from the shore, smoking, two points of orange light against the darkness of the forest.

The Indonesian archipelago loomed for a moment, dim and imminent, and then, more swiftly than Firuzeh thought possible, shrank to nothing.

CHAPTER SEVEN

Hassan's house was filled with boys making noise at all hours: boys clattering bowls, crushing cans, banging the tin sides of their home. Anyone might think they had twenty-two, not three.

Enough, Hassan said, flapping his hands. Go play in the graveyard.

The oldest two snatched up the metal cans they'd fashioned into incense burners and skipped off. The youngest stood sulking and picking his nose until Hassan pushed him out the door after them.

Have you heard from your brother? his wife said, flicking on the single bare bulb in their home. She opened her bag under the bulb and hunted through it.

Najib? He's fine, the new vines are strong and healthy—

You know which brother I mean.

Her hand closed on a small, grubby scroll of paper tied with white thread. She fished it out.

Hassan said: The family's probably halfway to Australia by now. Maybe he's there already and waiting to call.

He shrugged one arm into his coat, then the other. What's that trash you're playing with?

Nothing.

You better not be wasting our money on charms.

When you stop betting on chukar fights, I'll stop going to shrines to pray that you stop betting on chukar fights. She closed her hand, hiding the paper. Anyway, it's a traveler's charm.

Eh?

For safety. I wanted to give it to Bahar, but everything happened too fast. Maybe it will still work from here.

Superstitious nonsense, Hassan said, going to the door. Don't lose it.

Pick up bread on your way home.

Hassan walked down the mountain between houses that had mushroomed across its stony, tawny flanks almost overnight. Kabul was growing inexorably, grave by grave, office by wedding hall, swelling with the living and the dead. It was because of Omid's success that Hassan had moved his own family here from Parwan, and not a day passed now when he didn't curse Omid's auto shop, which was now Gorg Agha's auto shop, and utter heartfelt prayers for its ruination. A rocket would do, or an IED. Or, better, let an American soldier be shot in front of it.

Omid had struggled until his heart broke. And for what?

We'll marry your daughter to my son, Gorg Agha had said, while Omid was fixing his battered Corolla. Success should be shared with one's neighbors. And my son, he's on good terms with the Americans. Sells them alcohol. They'd investigate if he said, Oh, this neighbor might be an insurgent. Understand?

Can you believe it, Omid had said. It was Victory Day, and they were walking among the young and old trees in New City Park.

Hassan said: What did you think was going to happen? Abdul Rahman took our grandfather's rainlands in Ghor. Then there was Rabbani. Then the Taliban hunted us in the street. And you think you can rise up and be someone.

You sound like a Marxist.

You sound like a fool.

Is it a crime to dream?

You'll have to leave, Hassan said.

What? Why?

Do you think that if you give Gorg Agha your shop, he will stop there? He'll be back. He knows he can frighten your *no* into *yes*.

But where will we go? Omid said, eyes wide. Once, he had been a scab-kneed boy, no heavier than a sack of wheat. Once, Hassan had carried him on his shoulders.

I don't know, Hassan said. Anywhere. Wherever those leaving Afghanistan go. It's a country of exiles, of migrating swallows. They all must find someplace to rest. You will, too.

Unlike Omid, Hassan was bitter and wise. He worked for an old Tajik in a shop that made fences, welding and cutting and polishing until the sections were ready for display. Out in the sunlight, their chrome finish stung the eye. This was the best life that Hassan could hope for, the best life that his sons could hope for, and he chewed that pebble until his back teeth hurt.

Did you hear the news? the old Tajik said, as Hassan came in.

No, what news?

More schoolgirls poisoned. What's this world coming to? Don't leave your fingerprints on the metal. Wipe them off. Yesterday a customer complained.

All right.

No one wants grease on their shiny new fence. That's what they buy, Hassan. The shine, not the fence. We shine them so bright you can see the future in them.

Yes, Jamshed.

The fence says, You can keep death and misfortune out. Away from you and your family. You're rich, so rich you can have a fence like this, and you're not just rich, you're safe. You'll live longer than people without fences. All you have to do is spend a few thousand afghanis. What's money, anyway, when death comes knocking? Besides, I'm brighter than silver. If Hassan hasn't covered me in fingerprints.

I'll be more careful.

But you and I know that's a lie.

Sorry?

The truth: we have no future. Not me, not you. Not anyone.

Jamshed scratched his gray-haired ear.

Maybe the politicians. Maybe the very, very rich. But apart from them? Death comes when it wants to. Any day, there will be a bomb, or a bullet with your name on it, and you'll go to God.

But if you run far enough, Hassan said.

Even if you run all the way to Pakistan, death will find you. My cousin says they're kidnapping men right off the street. Better if I die in my homeland, he said. So he came home.

But if you go as far as Australia—

Where's that? Jamshed said.

30

Somewhere past India.

No, no. Death will find you anywhere. This isn't a fairy tale, Hassan. Pay a witch for a charm, say your prayers—save your money. Live realistically. And wipe your fingerprints off the finish.

So it looks like none of us ever existed and God Himself created this fence.

That's it exactly. That's what we sell.

CHAPTER EIGHT

The boredom, Nasima announced, was worse than the sharks. They had seen the fins at a distance the previous day, but now the water held only plastic bottles, chip bags, and snarls of seaweed.

Firuzeh volunteered that she preferred boredom.

Coward.

They were trapped by each other's legs and shoulders, prickly with splinters and stinging salt flakes. Atay and Abay took turns retching over the side from the boat's rolling and pitching. They had eaten fruit and Indomie noodles for three whole days. Then the fruit was gone, and they ate Indomie noodles day in and day out.

Firuzeh, promise me—

No.

At least hear me out!

Fine. But the answer's still probably no.

Promise me that wherever you go, you'll stay in touch.

Will they split us up?

I don't know.

Okay.

Okay what?

I promise.

Even if we end up on opposite sides of Australia. Write, or call, or send a pigeon or something.

We could end up as neighbors.

If you come to Perth. Which you should. It's the best place in Australia.

You've never been to Perth.

My brothers live there, stupid. And they told me about it. What do *you* know?

That you don't have many friends.

I'm too smart, that's why! Anyway, I have you. And I promise you won't get rid of me. Even if you move to the worst place in Australia. Even if you move to Adelaide.

Even if I wanted to get rid of you?

Nasima pinched her.

Ow!

So why did *your* family leave Afghanistan?

They won't tell me.

Won't tell you!

Abay says I don't need to know.

But you do! We need reasons like we need water or air. I'll be the best friend you ever had. I'll find you your reason. Look sweet, now. Smile.

What? Nasima, where are you—

Salaam, Uncle, Nasima said cheerfully, alighting on the other side of the boat. Firuzeh, numb and clumsy, scrambled after.

Mansour was sixteen or seventeen, he said when Nasima asked, though he looked older. The skin under his eyes had sunken into shadow.

Why was he on this boat?

His father.

What happened to his father?

He was arrested at gunpoint, stripped naked, and beaten. They returned to the house for Mansour, but his elderly neighbor had seen them coming and pounded on the door, gasping his warning. Mansour had leaped the rear wall just in time.

Where was his mother?

She had stayed.

What about you? Nasima said, hopping over outstretched feet. Why's someone like you on this ugly old boat?

You are little girls, Mr. Hassani said. Why do you ask about these things? You'll have bad dreams.

Firuzeh stammered until Nasima clapped a hand over her mouth. I have nightmares already, Nasima said. So, where are you from?

Iraq.

And why was Mr. Hassani, Iraqi, on this boat?

He had held political opinions.

Dangerous ones?

He'd been sent a warning.

Of what kind? A threatening phone call? An angry letter?

Mr. Hassani's brother.

His brother?

Most of him, anyway. So Mr. Hassani packed a bag and obtained, through a cousin, a fake passport, a plane ticket, and the number of a friend of a friend of the cousin's.

And you? Nasima said to Mr. Hassani's neighbor. Who are you?

I am Nobody.

Why are you here?

We were Mandaeans, in Iran.

We?

I have sons your age.

Then where are they?

We didn't have enough money to smuggle them too.

Mr. Nobody began to weep. Enormous tears rolled down his leathery cheeks and sank into his beard.

Firuzeh scooted backwards, the wood splintery against her feet.

Where are you going? Nasima cried. We're trying to figure out why *your* parents left. Which of these stories is like yours.

I don't want to know!

Abay laid a warm hand on Firuzeh's shoulder.

What have you been up to?

Nothing, Firuzeh said.

CHAPTER NINE

On their sixth day at sea, the typhoon came.

What had begun as a bruise along the horizon rapidly bled across the sky. The fishermen rolled the sails tight around their bamboo masts and nailed down the tarp the passengers had raised for shade. Every few minutes they looked over their shoulders at the approaching darkness. The wind smelled raw and alive.

The lucky ones who had gotten their hands on one of the boat's forty-odd life jackets checked and rechecked the battered plastic buckles. Firuzeh and her family had not been victorious in the scrum.

Soon, slanting streaks blurred the horizon.

Then the rain began.

Atay wrapped his arm around Firuzeh and pressed the two of them against the side of the boat. Abay did the same with Nour.

The smooth, untroubled water of the previous day now

heaved and fumed. A wave broke in pearls over the deck and hissed away. Salt spray whipped their faces. Around them, the other passengers wailed and prayed, their voices drowned out by the weltering water.

The boat leapt. Wood groaned.

The fishermen bailed with a bucket passed back and forth from the hold until the deck tilted and tossed the bucket holder to his knees. The bucket bounced once and vanished into the sea.

Then the rain closed its heavy curtains upon them, and Firuzeh could barely see past her nose.

Each breath Firuzeh drew was half water. As the boat pitched and yawed, she choked and gagged against Atay's tight hold. Every jolt against the boat's wood cut her skin, and the flying spray burned in the raw places.

By some unknown mercy, the nails and planks of the boat held together. When the storm finally dissolved to an insipid rain, the passengers were left chilled, stunned, and speechless. Atay's fist was so stiff that Abay had to rub the joints and blow on them before he could let go of Firuzeh's shirt. Nour shivered, teeth chattering. Around the boat, people wrung small creeks from their clothes.

Then the counting began.

Names wavered into the air. From one end of the boat, then the other, came answering calls and benedictions to God.

Nasima's mother came to them, stretching out her hands: Have you seen Nasima?

She must be somewhere, Atay said.

I let go of her—but she's a smart girl. She would have held on to something. Or maybe she went belowdecks. She's very bright. That must be where she is. I'll go see.

Have you seen Nasima? Rahmatullah Shahsevani asked on his third circuit of the deck. His voice had the thinnest of cracks in it.

No, but your wife went below to look.

Delruba emerged from the hold, swaying as if the storm still tipped and tilted the boat.

She wasn't down there? Rahmatullah said.

Keep looking! She might be hurt . . . She must be cold and afraid.

Who let go of her?

Who never held on? Nasima! Nasima, where did you go?

Enough, Rahmatullah Shahsevani said. He caught Delruba before she could fly belowdecks again. She bit his hand, and he shook her until her jaw slackened and clacked; and like that, the light and fury left her, and she sank to her knees on the deck and keened.

Abay rested one hand on Firuzeh's head and another on Nour's.

For two days and two nights, Nasima's mother beat her head and berated herself, her husband, and her absent sons, a lament broken only when sleep seized her here and there. Even then, she shook with hiccupping, whimpering sobs.

Nasima's father wilted.

No one slept for long.

The fishermen hung up wet maps to dry, consulted a compass, and cursed in their own language.

The whole boat was down to one meal a day. When Abay asked for water, she was refused. Firuzeh watched and listened.

But I'm hungry, Nour said. But I'm *thirsty*.

Rostam was hungry and thirsty too, Abay said. Heroes sometimes are.

During one of Delruba's lulls, Firuzeh dozed and dreamed that the boards of the boat parted, dropping her down and down, past silver sea serpents and streamers of kelp, to where the water was cold and black and heavy, so heavy it crushed the air from her lungs.

She gasped awake.

Hush. Abay pressed a hand to Firuzeh's forehead, then began to comb her tangled hair. Abay's hands were so gentle, Firuzeh barely felt the snarls.

Tell me a story, Firuzeh said.

All right. Mullah Nasruddin once had a donkey—

Not that sort of story.

What sort, then?

A story about Nasima.

Abay drew a breath.

I don't know if that is kind.

Khanem Delruba's asleep.

And if she wakes?

Then tell me a story about a girl like Nasima. Whose name might be Nasima, but we don't know.

Once there was a girl—

Who wore yellow leather shoes with daisies on them.

Who had yellow flowered shoes. And she, she went on a journey to find her brothers. An evil enchanter had come knocking on their door, his shadow long and bloody behind him. However, the boys had some magic of their own, and turned into doves and escaped. But they didn't take their sister with them. She was clever, though, and hid herself until the enchanter was gone, and marked which way her brothers flew.

Then she went after them, Firuzeh said.

Yes. She traveled for a long time, until her shoes were dusty and rotten with holes. At night when she slept, she could hear her brothers calling to her, because they were also lost and looking for her. They didn't mean to leave her behind, but they had been scared.

Like Nasima's mother calling Nasima's name. Over and over. So Nasima will hear and come back to her. Nasima can swim, you know.

Janam—

Does she find her brothers?

Of course she does, Nour said around the thumb in his mouth. This is Abay's story. If you want death and fighting and the good stuff, you have to ask Atay.

Shut up, Nour.

You shut up.

No, Abay said, putting the comb back into her bag. She finds them because a good sister will always find her lost brother. Or brothers. And the other way around. You remember that.

But Abay, Firuzeh said. What about your sisters and brothers? In Iran?

Land! came a cry: a dark figure at the prow, waving his arms, overcome. There's land, look!

And there was.

CHAPTER TEN

The boat's hull scraped, bumped, and crunched against coral, flinging them forward. Firuzeh, clambering upright, found that her hands and knees and skirt were wet.

We're sinking! Nour shouted, trying to plug the leaks with his toes.

One of the fishermen splashed over the side of the boat, stood up, and laughed. The sea, blue as Firuzeh's name, came up to his chest.

Other men jumped overboard as well and began wading to shore, balancing their few belongings on their heads. Atay joined them.

Come on, he said to Abay, beckoning. The water's warm.

She shuddered and hung back, pulling her scarf tight.

Fine, you can stay there, Atay said, splashing her. Nour! How about you?

Once he had ferried Nour to land on his shoulders, he returned for Firuzeh. She swayed while he carried her and tottered when he put her down. It was a sorry excuse for an island, she thought. A modest stretch of white coral sand ran upwards to sedges and a scattering of salt-bleached, sea-carved trees.

Behind her, Atay had succeeded in coaxing Abay into the water.

The fishermen brought the last seven packets of instant noodles and three jerry cans of water ashore. One by one, the remaining passengers flocked raggedly onto the beach. The boat, jammed nose-first in the sandbar, rocked softly with every wave. Most of its blue and yellow paint was gone. It seemed ready to spring apart at the lightest touch.

Atay and the other men conferred.

Race you! Nour shouted to the boys, and they were off, white sand fountaining in their wake.

Firuzeh followed more slowly, digging her toes deep. She kicked up a lump of something pale, porous, and light as air, then a tiger-striped nautilus the size of her head.

Water! Nour shouted. I found water!

By the time Firuzeh reached them at the well, Mansour had slapped Nour's cupped palms apart, droplets flying. The water was perfectly clear and cold, and she could see a long way down through the coral. But a sign with a skull and cross-bones hung over it.

You dummy, Firuzeh said, afraid.

I wouldn't have let him, Mansour said.

Nour said, But I'm thirsty!

We'll keep looking.

The island was not very large. Before long, Firuzeh spotted Atay and six other men near a rubber dinghy that had been hauled onto the beach, and on the far side of the dinghy, binoculars around their necks, three men and two women, pink and peeling from the sun.

The two groups stared at each other. Hello, Nour chirped, and all the boys echoed him. Hi. Hello.

Hello, said one of the pink women, who wore a shirt with white ferns on it and plastic flowers in her ears. She tried a few more sentences, waving her binoculars and flapping her arms, but stopped at their expressions of incomprehension. She turned and started to argue with her group. Then she put her shoulder to the dinghy and shoved it toward the water. With grimaces, the rest joined in.

Wait here, she mimed to Firuzeh and the others, as one pink man made the motor growl.

They waited, shuffling uncertainly, watching them go. The dinghy sputtered off through the turquoise water.

What kind of people are they?

Tourists.

Here?

No, you're right. They must be shipwrecked too.

Or lost.

But they have a boat.

You couldn't get far in that thing.

Before long, the dinghy reappeared. It puttered up into the shallows, and the woman in the fern shirt handed down a plastic jug of water and a fat canvas bag with twelve oranges inside.

Firuzeh did the math of twelve oranges for one hundred twenty-four people and swallowed, her throat dry.

The birders waved and smiled wide enough to show their molars, then spun up the grumbling motor and sped off.

When they returned to their landing point, Atay divided

the oranges into fractions, a taste to each person, then the orange peels as well. The children were allowed a mouthful of water each, which Firuzeh held in her mouth as long as she could, letting a few drops slide down her throat at a time.

This was not enough to ward off hunger.

Nor anger.

That night, as the fishermen stretched out on torn sails to sleep, the passengers surrounded them.

What is this place? Where are we?

Where's the food and water?

You brought us here to die!

Atay grabbed one fisherman by the shoulder and shook him. The fisherman grunted, rolled over, and plunged his fingers into his ears.

You have nothing to say? My son's crying from thirst!

Be patient, the oldest of the fishermen said in crumbs of Arabic. You thirst, we thirst. But a ship comes tomorrow.

You're lying.

Then kill me. But kill me tomorrow.

The oldest fisherman turned onto his stomach, pillowed his head on his arms, and almost immediately began to snore.

Firuzeh curled up on the grassy sand. Above her, stars she did not recognize blazed in the black vastness. A long time passed before she slept.

In the morning, a commotion.

There, Abay said, brushing sand from Firuzeh's hair. Southeast.

Nour yawned. What's going on? What's for breakfast?

Look.

Gray gleaming water slid over the beach and withdrew.

The sun burned gold and jagged on the waves, peppering Firuzeh's vision with green and purple blots. She squinted through the fence of her fingers and saw a sharp dark shape chipping the rim of the sky.

What's that?

Abay said: A ship.

From the Australian Navy, Atay added.

Nour leapt to his feet and danced, kicking sand in their faces. Atay lifted him up, his short legs still pedaling.

Any minute now, Atay said, radiant. Bahar, Nour, Firuzeh —we've reached Australia.

Fifteen at a time, the passengers were clipped into life jackets, loaded onto fiberglass boats, and conveyed to the ship. The sailors on the boats wore neat gray uniforms and crisp boots and would not look them in the eye.

A safe country—can you imagine? Abay hugged Firuzeh and Nour. No bombs. No checkpoints. No soldiers or Taliban.

Think of the house we'll live in, Atay said.

Oh, we don't need much. A bedroom, a stove—

Dream bigger than that. We're going to Australia.

A guest room? A garden. Omid, I want a garden.

And you'll have one, Atay said. I'll work harder than anyone. You'll live like Princess Soraya at home.

Don't talk nonsense, Abay said, laughing. What do you want, Firuzeh?

Firuzeh thought of Nasima. A friend. No, two friends.

I want a kangaroo! Nour shouted.

A black sailor raised one eyebrow at the familiar word. Kangaroos, you say? Bet you've never seen one before.

Kangaroo, yes! I want one! Where?

We've got loads, mate. Stick out your hand and you'll catch one.

Roy! Quit talking to the illegals and give me a hand here!

The sailor shrugged, winked at them, and went off to secure the lines.

Once the boats had been cranked aboard the ship and the passengers assembled beneath antennae as tall as trees, the sailors doled out water and dry rations. Careless of crumbs, Firuzeh crammed her mouth full and gulped water until she couldn't. The food sank into her belly and warmed and weighed her down.

When, some time later, the ship's enormous engines shut off, Atay had to carry her over the gangway, snorting and mumbling in her sleep.

CHAPTER ELEVEN

Fragments broke her sleep. The hollow sound of footsteps on a long dock, water clapping below. The familiar judder and rumble of a bus engine. A silvery web of fences parted to swallow them. Firuzeh blinked her eyes open, saw, and forgot.

When she woke up again, breathing air so humid it dewed her lips, she was in a tent, on a bunk that quivered and creaked. A hanging sheet partitioned their side from—she flicked the sheet aside—a Sri Lankan family's.

Firuzeh stepped outside and saw rows of canvas tents, a single tree writhing up among them, and a fence running as far as the eye could see.

Where are we? she said. Is this Australia?

If it is, Nour said, Australia is very ugly.

Atay said, This is Nauru. We're not in Australia yet.

Naur-o? Nour-u?

Yes, an island of your own.

We have to wait a bit longer, Abay said.

How long? Nour said.

Only a few days, I'm sure, Atay said. Then you'll see your kangaroos.

The bunks wobble, Firuzeh said.

It's too hot, Nour said.

And—agh—there's mosquitoes!

Abay said, Look! You can see the ocean from here. Why don't we think of this as a vacation? Like we're rich and on holiday—just for a few days.

Like how that fishing boat was supposed to be a cruise ship? Firuzeh said, flattening another mosquito against her arm.

Nour let a hungry one settle on him. Mansour says the fence is fresh. He says this place smells like money, and that means we'll stay here forever. Why does he say that if we're leaving soon?

Atay said, That silly boy. He argued when they were collecting our mobiles. They had to push him against the wall, like a criminal, to take away his. Only thinking about himself. We can't let them form bad opinions of us—

Abay said, After what that boy's lived through, he imagines dark things easily. That's all.

Atay said, You shouldn't be hanging around Mansour. He'll get into trouble sooner or later.

For dinner, they followed a stream of bodies to the mess tent, where they sat down on plastic chairs at a plastic table to eat, with plastic forks that twisted and bent when applied. Everyone received square white slices of bread and lumps of leathery chicken.

If only I had a tandoor, Abay sighed. Even a pan. She gave one slice of her bread to Nour, and he stuffed it in his mouth.

These chickens must have been bored out of their brains, Firuzeh said, chewing and chewing. You can taste it.

Have I raised you to talk about your food like that?

We'll be out soon, Atay said. In a few weeks, maybe.

Nour said: Abay, are you still eating?

Abay handed him her plate, and Nour dug in.

Let's go wash, Abay suggested, when they were all done.

Strangers pointed the way to the ablutions block: down a row of tents, then a left, then a right. The lines stretching out of each door dissolved as they approached. Men and women groused in various languages. One small boy held up his shirt and squatted right there.

A thick stink surrounded them. The air effervesced with flies.

What's the matter? Abay called out.

A woman shouted back: No water!

That can't be right.

See for yourself.

Firuzeh followed her mother into the sour ablutions block, stepping carefully across the slick cement.

Abay jerked at the tap handles, one after another, spinning all four pairs loose. No water flowed. She stared at them.

No water—

I miss Kabul, Firuzeh said as they returned to their tent.

Don't say that.

You could pump water on the street—

Abay stooped for a handful of sandy soil and rubbed it briskly between her fingers.

See? she said. Good enough for now. Only a month or so until they take us to Australia.

At midnight, guards barged into their tent, swinging torch beams.

Up! they barked. Head count! SHU 106, 107, 108, 109!

Here, Atay said, rubbing sleep from his eyes. The guards snorted, shoved aside the sheet, and stormed into their neighbors' section.

At 6 a.m., their torches blazed into the tent again.

Wake up! Head count!

Midnight.

2 a.m.

6 a.m.

Midnight.

They're like robots, Nour said. They never sleep.

They have shifts, stupid.

Shut up, SHU 107.

You shut up, SHU 106.

CHAPTER TWELVE

Every day the bread and rice and chicken.

Every night, Firuzeh flinched awake at 2 a.m., whether the guards had come or not. Then she lay still, her heart pounding, for hours.

For the same reason, she rarely slept past six. It was difficult to keep her eyes open during the day, but the heat made napping miserable.

She missed school, and the crisp taste of Kabuli onions and grapes, and the balloon man dragging his painted bouquet. She missed Sheringol and Homaira and even the boys who shied rocks at her after school, as punishment for knowing too many right answers.

Deep lines wore into Abay's face. Atay grew hoarse in his declarations of impending departure, until one day he fell abruptly silent.

The days passed, gray and indifferent.

CHAPTER THIRTEEN

Upon their resettlement in Australia, Jawed and Khairullah had first bunked in a nine-person flat, three men to a room, with people coming and going constantly, so the two beds in each room never cooled. For all its noise, for all that they had to pass sideways in the corridor, that flat had been fitted with a precious landline. The residents dropped coins into the jar beside the phone whenever they called home, wherever home was.

Then there had been a three-person flat, a quieter and easier place to sleep, where Jawed and Khairullah shared a prepaid mobile. Once a week, between construction jobs, they called home and told Nasima about the shops that sold lollies in every colour, and the brilliant blue water of the Indian Ocean, like a great jewel set in a bezel of white sand. They assured their parents and were reassured in turn that the entire family was in good health, no troubles at all. Then the boys told their parents how much to expect that week.

It was Khairullah, the older one, who had the idea of buying a package of lollies each time one or the other had a dollar to spare. Box by box and bar by bar, they assembled a small wall of sweets in their room. Every time Khairullah added a Violet Crumble or a bag of strawberry clouds to the pile, he put his fists on his hips and laughed.

I can see her now, he said, can't you?

When Nasima arrived, she would rip wrappers and tear apart paper boxes, eating until her tongue was striped green and blue and her upper lip smeared with chocolate.

Jawed, three years younger than Khairullah, examined the expiration dates, and when they were a day or two away, would bring the chocolate bar or Cherry Ripe to his brother and pull a pleading face.

Oh, all right, Khairullah always said. They split the lollies between them, tasting tart partedness on their tongues.

The last call thrummed their mobile while they were on the bus to work.

We're leaving, Nasima said breathlessly; then their father commandeered the phone.

Thank you for the money, he said. Do not send any more. We've made arrangements with the man who smuggled you. All of us will join you in Australia, in that place you said— Perth. We'll call when we go.

Two days later, Jawed dropped their mobile into the sea.

Khairullah had suggested they walk the fifteen kilometres from Scarborough to their flat in Mosman Park to save on fares. Jawed had resisted, then insisted on taking the beach, never mind the sand infiltrating their shoes and gritting the skin between their toes. The water gleamed turquoise and tourmaline.

Within ten minutes Jawed had run onto one of the rocky moles that jutted out into the sea, whooping and leaping like a man possessed. On either side of him, waves flung up fans of feathery lace. Water pooled in the hollows of the barnacled rocks. Jawed turned to Khairullah, arms wide.

Then his foot skidded. He slipped and splayed. The mobile slid from his pocket, rebounded off a rock, and fell into the sea.

Ah, fuck, Jawed said, feeling his bruised bum. Another wave shattered over him, and spray dripped in rivulets down his dark hair.

Khairullah advanced onto the rocks, legs locked, hands braced for a fall. The sight of so much water still frightened him.

Idiot! he shouted. Are you hurt?

Ooh, it hurts everywhere.

I'll—I'll come get you. Khairullah edged forward along the mole, prodding each algal rock to test its slickness.

Nah, I'm fine.

Jawed crawled to his feet and hobbled and hopped to his brother.

Nothing broken?

Nope. But I lost the mobile.

You lost the—

Didn't you see? Boop, oop! There it went. It's a shame about the credit, I think we had seventy-five cents left.

Khairullah punched him in the gut. He doubled over.

Agh! What was that for?

Did *you* write down Baba's number anywhere?

It's on the phone—oh.

And when they call the number they have for us again—

Maybe a fish will pick up, Jawed said.

Even if we had the money. Which we don't. Even if we

bought and loaded a new mobile straightaway. How in the world would we call them?

Won't they be travelling for a while? They might not even think to call.

They said they'd call right before they left.

Oh. Right.

Now they'll think we're, what, dead? In prison? Sick? Hurt?

Maman will think all those things at once. She'll fling her hands over her face and wail, O my children! Is there no God? Sick, hurt, dead, and imprisoned! How much can a mother bear?

You have no right to make jokes, Khairullah said. You've lost our mobile and Baba's number.

What, do you want me to dive for it? Lala, I don't want to. The water's cold.

Khairullah folded his arms and thought. We'll have to hope they try the old number. And that someone at the flat figures it out. Do we have Zaman's contact?

Yes, I saved it on the phone.

Khairullah kicked a vicious arc of sand.

It's like they're in space, and we've lost the signal, he said. They can't reach us. We can't reach them. So how—

I'll take a bus to our old place, Jawed said, squeezing his brother's shoulder. Someone will remember me. I'll ask them to tell Baba if he calls. And to write down his number and give it to us.

They still have to think of calling the old place.

They will. Before they call a funeral director, at least.

What did I say about joking, eh?

I'm serious!

Fine. And if you weren't being serious?

I'd say we buy all the chocolate in Perth and put it in a pile. Nasima will find us by the smell. Straight across the ocean, dragging the boat. Hello troublemakers, where are the lollies you promised me?

She must have grown.

What if she's grown as tall as your chin? Or taller! What if she grows taller than you?

Then she's eating well. I'll punch anyone who complains.

The dunes on their left bristled with spinifex and saltbush, striped here and there with paths to the road. Glowering rain clouds stitched themselves to the sea. They walked side by side, Jawed whistling, Khairullah staring west through the clouds, past the heartbreaking blue of the ocean. He looked until he saw the whitewashed rooms of the family home, and the trees in the compound—a crooked almond and a spreading pear—and a little girl climbing into the pear for a nestful of speckled eggs.

They'll find us, Khairullah said, shivering. They must.

Is that rain?

Let's walk faster.

When they had gone, a raindrop fell and cratered the white sand. Then another. Soon the double line of footprints washed away.

CHAPTER FOURTEEN

One hot, feverish, humming night, Firuzeh turned over and over on the lower bunk, trailing her fingers in the dirt, then flinging an arm over her sweaty face. Her clothes pinched and chafed. The blanket itched. When a mosquito sang beside her ear, she thrashed at it.

You know, Nasima said, I feel bad for you.

The drowned girl sat on the side of the bunk, face pale in the gloom, as if she wore her own scrap of moonlight. Her hair was wet and braided with kelp, pinned here and there with fishbone combs.

The mosquito whined again. Firuzeh slapped her pillow. Hey, you're the one who died.

I went quick. You'll take ages.

She laid a cool hand against Firuzeh's cheek.

I mean look at you.

Did you come just to gloat about dying?

I would never. We're friends, Firuzeh. You forgot, but I promised. I wanted to see how you were doing.

Now you know. You should go to your parents. They miss you. They never stop talking about you.

I tried, Nasima said, but they didn't see me. Like when I was alive. I was a daughter-shaped space in the universe. You feed it. You put shoes and dresses on it. You raise it properly, like a sheep, so you can take it to market someday. But you don't see her, you don't see your daughter, not really. Not the way you see your sons. Who are worth something. Who'll work someday.

So why can I—

You saw through the bullshit. Plus, you don't really think I'm dead.

Of course you're—

So why tell yourself stories about girls named Nasima who have adventures on the seafloor?

Nasima laughed, a low and watery sound.

You kept me awake with your loud bright dreams.

I didn't mean to.

They eyed each other, Firuzeh damp with sweat and the blood of crushed mosquitoes, Nasima dripping and steaming with seawater.

Can you go back—to sleep? Firuzeh ventured. Can I—is there anything I can—

Oh, I'm not ready to forgive you yet. But *you* can go back to sleep.

Nasima reached out and pressed a finger against Firuzeh's left eyelid, then the right.

There. That's as much as I can do for you.

What—Firuzeh yawned—what did—

CHAPTER FIFTEEN

There's a bus, Abay said. Her foot tapped the packed earth.

Firuzeh glanced away from the beetle creeping along her bunk. A bus?

What good is a bus? Atay said. What we need is a boat.

A plane, Nour begged. Please, no more boats.

A bus to *town*, Abay said. That I can ride. We need things —have you seen our daughter's shoes?

They all looked at Firuzeh, who flushed. On her right foot, the seam in the fake leather had opened, and the shoe's upper flapped like a mouth full of toes.

And with what money will you buy our daughter shoes? Atay said.

At this, Abay undid the knots in her skirts and performed magic tricks between the mattress and bunk, conjuring a respectable mound of coins.

Dishwashing, she explained, when there's water. And helping with odds and ends in the kitchen. It's not much—

Jewel among women, Atay said, and kissed her forehead. We'll go to town!

Yes, well. The bus leaves tomorrow. That's the only time this week. But I'm supposed to be washing dishes after lunch. So if you, dear, dear husband, could—

Take the children to town?

—report to the kitchen at half past noon. Say you're my husband. That would mean another few cents for us. You put me in charge of the household for a reason, she added. When you bargain, the price goes *up*.

And the children?

Will stay here. And keep out of trouble. It's not easy to get on that bus, Abay said, vanishing the coins one by one. There's a lottery.

Take Nour, at least. So he can look out for you. You'll be a man for your mother, won't you?

Yes, Atay, Nour said.

But— Firuzeh said.

He can sit in your lap, Atay said.

That's true—

It shouldn't be a problem.

Firuzeh said again, But what about—

I know your shoe size. I can take one with me, to be sure. Maybe we'll get an ice cream, Nour, if you behave. Would you like that?

Nour squealed and hopped from foot to foot.

Firuzeh crossed her arms, slouched, and seethed.

CHAPTER SIXTEEN

Up up up, Nour, Abay sang, sweet as a bulbul. We're going to
town and the bus won't wait.

Nour squirmed in Abay's arms as she wiped his face. Always smudges on his chin. One of the mysteries of small boys.

Firuzeh would never wriggle and yelp. Firuzeh knew better. If she was getting a cold sweet suck of ice cream, she
would have earned it through good behavior—she would
never kick Abay's arm like that.

Once the two of them left the tent, taking the injustice of
their joy with them, Firuzeh dressed herself with deliberate
slowness, as befitted someone on an important errand, more
important than shoes and ice cream. Then she devoted herself
to kicking a stick around the fenced perimeter of the camp.

The stick scribbled snakes in the dust as she went. One,
two, three. The sun baked dark the back of her neck like
bread.

It never mattered that Firuzeh had been top of her class; or that she sometimes listened, maybe even half the time, when Abay and Atay asked her to be quiet and stop singing; or that she only pinched Nour or pulled his hair when he really, truly, and deeply deserved it. No one struck medals for her sacrifices. No one even mentioned them. Nour got the fussing and the kisses, the ice cream and sweets.

Mosquitoes hummed in her ears. The tents fluttered drably.

From one of the tents came mewling and low grunting and a rhythmic thump and creak. Firuzeh paused, then lifted the tent flap with her stick.

A man lay atop a woman in a lower bunk, his trousers pleated around his ankles, her dress frilling to either side. They clutched each other as though they were drowning, and the sounds they made were sounds of grief.

When the woman opened her eyes, her face red, she saw Firuzeh. Cursing in a language Firuzeh did not know, she plucked up a sock beside the bunk and hurled it.

Firuzeh ducked the missile and fled.

Once there was a mullah who ate all the ice cream he wanted, she said to herself, but she could not imagine how to continue the story. She squatted in the shade of the glossy-leaved tree at the center of camp, ignoring the men playing cards nearby, and wrote glyphs and hexes in the dust with her stick.

Once there was a mother who went to buy shoes for her daughter, but without the daughter, and she bought shoes that were too small or too large, none the right size—wasn't she sorry when she came home! Once a man and a woman drowned in each other's eyes on dry land, and no one could figure out how they died.

Little girl, your stories are all beginnings! one of the card players said. Those aren't stories. What happens next to your mullah? To your mother?

I don't know.

Say: Some days and some while passed. That is how my mother told stories. Then tell me something magical. A wonder. A feat. Tell me that the wicked are punished or that the foolish find wisdom. Lastly, you must say: They stayed on that side of the water, and we on this.

If you're playing, play, one of his companions said. Don't bother the girl with your silliness.

The first man nodded encouragement to Firuzeh. Go on, try again. One day among days—

Some time and some while passed, she said, frowning. The Australians stayed on that side of the water, and we on this.

The card players broke into raucous laughter.

See what you did there, Mahmoud.

She's a smart one.

Clever.

Where's your father, little girl?

Excuse me, Firuzeh told them. I have to go.

The bus disgorged its riders one by one. They clutched their purchases to their chests, their expressions grim. Firuzeh stood on tiptoe but could not see Abay or Nour in the thinning crowd.

Omid's wife, she heard. Trouble. Someone should tell him.

Nour bumped down the bus steps then, a ring of ice cream around his mouth, his eyes white all around. He ran to Firuzeh and clamped himself around her waist, holding so tightly it hurt.

What's wrong? Firuzeh said. Where did Abay go?

Nour buried his face in her stomach.

There was a soft thumping, like a moth beating against a windowpane.

Abay's face flashed in the bus window, her mouth a circle, her hands scratching and scrabbling at the glass. Two moths.

The bus door folded shut. The bus coughed a tubercular cough, then wheeled around and lumbered out through the camp's silver gates. The gates clashed together behind it.

Sandals slapped the dust. Atay was there, panting, doubled over, hands pressed to his knees.

Where is your mother? he said, and Firuzeh pointed through the gates at the vanishing bus and the long yellow plume of dust behind it. The bus turned a bend in the road and was gone.

Your mother didn't get off the bus?

She tried, Firuzeh said.

Nour, what happened? Nour, be brave for me, tell me—Nour—

Nour pressed his lips together, shook his head, and sobbed sugar and snot into Firuzeh's shirt. However they begged and pleaded with him, he refused to say another word.

Khalil had been on that bus. Firuzeh had seen him. He was a sullen pock-faced boy who shoved his hands in his pockets to hide whatever he had recently filched. Nour horsed around with him sometimes. Although he could not have been much older than Firuzeh, he was in the camp alone.

She watched him while they ate.

The boy he always sat with, Payam, finished eating his dinner and left.

Nour picked listlessly at his plate. Atay swept his arms wide, demanding answers no one would give. God only knows, someone said; others chewed and glanced meaningfully at the children.

After Khalil stood to go, Firuzeh pleaded a stomachache and followed him.

In a dark row between tents, she grabbed Khalil by the wrist.

Tell me.

I don't know anything.

Liar.

Ask Nour.

He won't talk to anyone. Tell me.

No.

A moment later, he was sprawled in the dust, pinned and struggling under her greater weight. Firuzeh raised her arm to hit him again.

Wait, he said. I'll tell you.

Khalil's sandals had fallen to pieces. He had been borrowing a pair that his small feet wallowed in. When his name came up in the lottery, he thought it a fantastic stroke of luck.

So I went to the shop, he said, and the shopkeeper glared—wouldn't take his eyes off me, not the whole time I was there—

You're babbling, Firuzeh said. Tell me about Abay.

You have to be back on the bus by three. She was late.

What happened?

Maybe Nour didn't want to come back. Town's nice. Maybe she didn't know the rules. Does it matter?

Keep going.

Ten minutes late, the guard said. He had a watch. She was

the last one on the bus. I didn't look at her. None of us did. I had my shoes. She was none of my business.

Some man you are. If I was there—

But you weren't.

Shut up and keep talking.

He made a face at her. Pick one.

She balled her hand into a fist.

The guard said, we thought you ran away. She said, where on earth would I run? He said, do you know what happens to detainees who are late?

What?

A long night in Seg.

What does that mean?

Your mother asked, too. No one told her. We were ashamed. We got to the camp, and the guard said, get out! She said, help me. I got off the bus. She said, help me, please, in the name of God. No one did. You can hit me now.

CHAPTER SEVENTEEN

Quentin Marks was a proud Queensland battler, born of battlers, who could trace his family tree back to a forger on one of the very first convict ships. That illustrious ancestor had owned an engraved silver pocket watch, which was now on display in a national museum.

Quentin had poured beers in dive bars, picked veg, and washed oysters on a pearl boat, but something in his bones told him that this was the job he'd tell stories about. It was adventure and good money, more zeros in his salary than he'd ever seen, and at twenty-two, with Ella up the duff and the grim gulf of serious responsibilities yawning, Quentin desperately needed the cash. He'd only be gone a year, he told her, year and a half at most, herding the illegals on Nauru the way her uncle herded cattle. Then he'd come home to church her properly, with all the fancies and fairy floss a woman like her deserved. After that, he'd learn to lay roofing or tiles, and they'd rent a house of their own, with a yard for the kiddos.

If Nauru was a blessing for Quentin, it was the blackest of curses for the brown boat scum. They had been promised freedom and the Australian dole, not tropical heat and tents and endless fences. You could see the rage and betrayal in their eyes, and it made you put a hand on your baton. But this job was decent enough, even though the town was a bit poky. Even though all the island women were fat.

Today he was on office duty, guarding sanitary pads and shaving razors with his life.

"Back again?" he said to the Iraqi woman hovering at the donga's door. She was a picture of embarrassment. "Weren't you just here three hours ago?"

She turned even redder—if such a thing were possible—snatched the soft package from his hand and vanished.

No bloody sense of humour.

Next up was an Afghan gent who pantomimed at his yellow teeth. "Please."

"You can have a toothbrush if you can say the word proper. Tooth. Brush."

"Tootebrosh."

"Nah, mate. Toothbrush."

"Toot-e-*brosh*."

"And you people think you can make a go of it in Australia. Christ." He surrendered the toothbrush. "Hey, don't go. What do you say now?"

"*Toot*-e-brosh."

"No, no, you're supposed to say *Thank you for the toothbrush*. Courtesy of the Australian federal government. Hotelier for illegals and detainees. So let's hear it."

"Tank you. For toot-e-brosh."

"Christ."

Desk duty would be deadly dull if he, Quentin Marks, didn't have a heart of gold, a love of laughs, and a deep concern for the welfare of his charges. Even if they were all deported tomorrow to whatever hellholes they had crawled out of, learning a spot of English would do them good. Maybe it would save their lives someday. He could see it now: that gentleman racing after a disguised terrorist into the lobby of the Intercontinental, stretching out his finger in accusation, and proclaiming, with perfect enunciation, "The toothbrush! The *toothbrush*!" Whereupon the smartly uniformed concierge would wrestle the terrorist to the ground and discover the tiny ticking incendiary device secreted in his hollowed-out Super Soft Triple Action with Gum Massager. The tourists whose lives had been saved by that gent's warning would organize a collection for him. And he would clasp his hands with astonished gratitude and say, in crisp, clear English, "Thank you. Thank you all so much. But thank you most of all to Mr Quentin Marks, who taught me English in the detention camps. Now there's a good bloke."

Grinning at the thought, Quentin shuttered the office and waved to Peter and Beth, who were on gate duty. They punched the button to let him through.

It had been a quiet day, and that was all right. He made the same money on quiet days as on riot days, and while there was a certain thrill in donning helmet and kneepads, bashing baton against plexiglass shield, and watching detainees' faces transform from rage to fear—he shivered with pleasure at the memory from training on Christmas Island—it could not be denied that the gear was heavy and hot, in a climate where you broke a sweat if you farted.

Quiet was easy, and Quentin liked easy. Tonight, for example, would be an easy night. A cold stubby at his hotel to start, then dinner at the Chinese restaurant. Maybe a quick call home to Ella.

The bartender, a native with the paunch to prove it, was uncharacteristically glum tonight.

"Ah, Lionel, suffering from a spot of guilt? This stuff's half water, I knew it. Doesn't taste like anything we've got at home."

"Mr Marks, they're talking about shutting the detention centre down."

"Oh? And who's feeding you that bull?"

"Your PM on the telly, sir."

"Well, wouldn't you like that? All the illegals off your nice island, no more worrying about the missus in the case of a riot."

"But there'd be no business. We haven't had a tourist in years. No detention centre, no hotel—no bar. And then what?"

"Ah, don't talk like that. I'd lose my job too, you know. We'd make the best of it. My mum's rabid about shipping them all back, you should hear her bollocking her MP. What about you, she says to me, you have to watch those shitheads all day. Don't you want them to bugger off back to the desert? Not until I'm done with this job, I tell her. Don't forget, they're paying my bills."

"Mine, too," Lionel said, and poured him a drink.

"Hey, you," Beth said. "Shove over, mate."

"How's the old summer camp holding up in my absence?"

"A riot a minute. We're missing the fun. VB, please."

"All out, madam. Sorry."

"Aw, but they promised they'd call if there's fun."

74

"Nah, Marks. It's been dull as a dunny. No, I lie, there's one refugee carrying on something awful. I'm surprised we can't hear him from here. He's that loud. His wife's been popped into jail for the night. To hear him, you'd think we'd murdered her."

"Got the red-carpet treatment, I suppose?"

"Did it myself. What an eyeful. The tits on those people, they're huge—like biscuits. No wonder he's throwing such a fit. Anyway, one night in there in the nuddy and she'll think twice before holding up the bus again."

"Our prison is famous for its mosquitoes," Lionel said. "Would madam like a Corona instead?"

"Sure thing."

Ella was a bit lonely at home, but fine.

"Chundering like nobody's business," she said, "but at five months, what do you expect."

"Could be worse," he said. "You could be living in a place like this. We have pregnant women in the camp—can you imagine? Some have been here for six months, eight months, a year."

"They'd have had to—"

"In the boats, yeah, and in the tents here."

"Yuck."

"Nature finds a way."

"You could write a book about it someday."

"You mean, the job?"

"That, yeah."

Quentin considered it. He was not a literary man, but the idea of the Marks family history between tooled leather covers—now *that* was an appealing thought. And wasn't his own life one long adventure, the kind that kids read about on farms so far apart that teachers held classes over radio? Now this was a proper Australian story, the girl or boy would say, staring out over miles of yellow grass and red dust and dreaming of pearl boats and detention-camp riots.

Someone ought to write it, that was for sure.

CHAPTER EIGHTEEN

A long night passed, and then a long day, the longest in their forgetfully numbered months on the island. Abay's absence, mother-shaped, sat with them at dinner, walked with them to the tent, and lay down on her bunk.

Atay sat. He stood. He paced the tent. He sat again, then sprang to his feet. In his restless hands, an unwashed shirt gritted and tore, strip by strip and thread by thread.

Nour hooked his knees to his nose and squinched his eyes shut.

Go to sleep, Atay said. I'm going for a walk.

I talked to Khalil, Firuzeh whispered to Nour.

She snaked up from her bunk until she peeped over his.

Well what do you have to say for yourself?

His hands pulled at each other.

It should have been me. I wouldn't have made Abay late.

Firuzeh slipped back into her bunk. Looked up. Hissed at the slight sinking swell of wire where her brother's weight was:

Your fault.

In the dark, in the silence, it was harder to ignore the Abay-absence sitting there as heavy as a living thing. Breathing in and out. Watching.

Atay did not return. The tent flap blew in and out with the night breeze.

Firuzeh turned away from Abay's bunk until the pillow grew hot under her cheek, then turned back, then rolled over again and pretended to sleep, so Nour at least would know she had nothing on her conscience, no, nothing at all. None of this was her fault. It just went to show—

The dip in the upper bunk from his balled-up body never changed.

She flopped out her limbs, abandoning the pretense of sleep.

Say something, donkey.

—

I know you're awake.

—

Firuzeh puffed out her cheeks. Fine.

The bunk bed squeaked and rocked as she climbed up, its metal almost cool against the soles of her feet. She punched her brother's shoulder.

Hey.

—

Do you want me to tell you a story? Will that get you to fall asleep?

Nour's eyes rose above the two hills of his knees. You're not Abay.

And you're not Rostam, but who's checking?

You're a bad sister.

Nour's nose now emerged.

Khalil has two sisters and they're terrible, he says, but I'd rather have them than you. If it wasn't for you, we wouldn't be here. If it wasn't for your shoes, Abay wouldn't be in jail.

But she is. We are. Here I am. At least you got to go to town. At least you ate ice cream. Now, I know you like mullah stories, Nour. Listen. Once they asked the mullah why he always answered questions with questions. He chewed on his beard and said, Do I?

That's not a good story.

Maybe you don't know what a good story is.

Maybe you're bad at telling stories.

Okay. Here's another. One time the mullah was rowing a ferry, and a scholar came and asked to cross—

No, Nour said. No more mullah stories.

What kind of story, then?

An exciting one.

All my stories are exciting, onionhead.

No, they're not.

You try.

Make it about a boy, Firuzeh. That'll make it exciting. Boys grow up to be heroes. Soldiers. Kings. Girls—well, you get married. And that's boring.

All right, little sultan. A boy. How old?

Seven. And he's brave. He's never afraid.

Where does he live?

A village. But he can see the whole world if he climbs on the roof. He climbs up there all the time because he's not afraid of heights. He keeps goats. When wolves and bandits try to steal them, he beats them up. He's not afraid of anything.

What are his parents like?

He was found on the mountain as a baby. No one knows where he came from.

Does he have a sister?

No. He has pigeons. The fastest, prettiest pigeons. When he whistles, they fly all over, then tell him everything they see. Where greedy men hide their gold. When wolves come for the goats. How close the war is. If anyone died.

Is there a war?

There's always a war, Firuzeh. What a stupid question.

So, once there was a boy, who was everything you said. One day he leaves the village—

No.

No what?

The boy doesn't leave the village. He doesn't walk to the city. The village is home. He knows everyone there, even the mean old man, with red-eyed dogs, who glares at him and yells and spits.

How does he go on adventures if he never leaves home?

Maybe he doesn't need adventures.

Maybe. But like you said, there's a war. Maybe one day he climbs up on the roof and sees that the fighting is close—

No, that doesn't happen. That never happens. He's safe. He and the whole village are safe. His pigeons are always watching, always telling him, and they never see the war come close. Every day the villagers crowd his door, even the mean old man, and they ask him, where's the fighting? Should we run? And every day he says, it's far away. We're safe. So they never have to pack their bags and leave.

Is that it?

He always wins at walnuts and hopping fights. Sometimes he loses on purpose, so the other children don't feel bad, but he could win if he wanted.

Anything else?

Oh, he wears a coat and boots made of wolfskin. From all the wolves he's killed, just him and his stick. That's everything.

And they stayed on that side of the water, and we on this.

See, now that was a good story.

Nour smacked his lips, yawned, and stretched out on his bunk.

Firuzeh? The ice cream—it didn't really taste good.

She patted his curls. Little liar, she said.

Wispily, Nour began to snore.

If Firuzeh looked too long into the darkness of Abay's bunk, it threatened to split open and swallow her.

Nour was asleep. Their neighbors on the other side of the sheet were asleep. She could feel her heart knocking against the bars of her bones.

Somewhere outside, Atay was walking long lonely circles under the watchlights and the moon.

Firuzeh said: Nasima.

I'll tell you a secret, the drowned girl said.

Nasima pulled a pearl from under her tongue and rolled it between her fingers.

Your parents can't save you. And you can't save them.

Liar.

Tell me how you'll save Abay. Tell me how Abay could possibly save you. When the waves are high and the boat is spinning, spinning . . .

Just because your mother let go doesn't mean—

The sharks eat the bodies, Nasima said. So many boats. So many storms. For a little while the bodies float. Then they sink. But they never reach the bottom.

But you survived, Firuzeh said. And Abay will get out. We'll make it to Australia.

Nasima said: Mothers, lovers, little boys, old men, uncles. All drowned. All falling. The storm water roils, rough and high, but below that you fall slowly. Flesh fraying. Traps of white teeth tearing and taking.

Firuzeh said: You're telling a story.

I saw what I saw.

CHAPTER NINETEEN

Breakfast, variously glutinous and stale, had no appeal for any of them. They went to the mess tent out of habit, Firuzeh thumbing the white pebble she'd found under her pillow.

Atay sat like a stone.

Firuzeh tore and mashed her bread and pushed the pieces around her plate.

Nour rolled bread pellets and flicked them off his spoon. One bounced off of Firuzeh's nose.

Feery-zeery, what are you doing today?

Catching a big beetle and pulling off its wings.

Can I help?

No, go catch your own.

Nour swelled up. Then I'll catch a turtle.

What do you want with a turtle?

All kinds of things. I can build a twig city on the back of its shell. Flip it so it kicks upside down in the air. Hide it in Atay's clothes so he yells. And when you come asking if you can play with it too, I'll tell you to go catch your own.

You better hurry up and start looking, then.

You watch. Hey, Khalil! Let's find a turtle! Atay, can I go?

Atay blinked. Half a nod. Nour shot off.

Azad, whose beard was full of crumbs, leaned over the long table and said, Remember that God is merciful. To me and to you.

Does this look like mercy?

What is and isn't mercy is determined by God.

Tell that to Bahar. Do you dare? What they've done to her, what they're doing now, I can't imagine—I don't want to. All night and all day I've been trying not to think.

All God wants is for us to submit.

Haven't I submitted? Hasn't my whole life been one punch in the mouth after another? At what point am I allowed to fight?

Never, Azad said. But justice comes in its own time.

You've gone mad, Atay said. It's the weather. This heat.

I'll leave you alone. Only—Omid—please, don't jump the guards. I can see it in your face. There's a look a man gets. They'll bring Bahar back, and you'll be gone. What would be the good in that?

There's no good anywhere. Not in heaven. Not on earth.

Firuzeh cleared her throat.

Besides my children, Atay amended, ruffling her hair. Weren't you going to find a beetle?

Do beetles eat this bread, Atay?

They're all this bread is good for. So, why not? What'll you do when you catch it, janam?

Lock it up in Segregation.

Atay stared. What?

A plastic bag, maybe, or one of Nour's shoes.

Why?

I need to know if it escapes. If Abay—

I advise you to keep your mind off it, Azad said.

Shit on your mother, what do you think I've been trying to do? Be a good girl, Firuzeh, and look after Nour.

I'm always good, Firuzeh huffed, and went.

Five beetles later, their lacquered shards and comb-toothed legs littering the ground around her, Firuzeh heard the rattle and wheeze of the bus. She left her sixth victim twitching three-legged in the dust and ran.

Fast as she was, Atay was faster. By the time she reached the bus, he had Abay supported on his shoulder, his arm wrapped around her.

Nour careened into them, tripping Atay. He pushed his wet face into Abay's skirt. Part of Firuzeh wished to do the same. But she was grown and good.

Abay did not look at them.

We've learned a lesson today, haven't we, a blonde guard said with a smile.

Quick as a snake, Nour lunged at her. His nails clawed at the coarse cloth of her uniform without finding purchase. He sat, sank his teeth in her leg, and held on.

She screamed.

Firuzeh laughed.

Other guards came running, radios fizzing, nightsticks out. Firuzeh bent to Nour, who bounced and jolted as the guard kicked, and wrapped her arms around him.

Let go! she shrieked in English, pretending to pull. In Dari, she whispered to him: Hang on tight.

The first blow stung her shoulder like a wasp.

The second thumped into her ribs.

The third swing cracked against her skull. Her arms went slack, and she spilled sideways into the dirt.

They pulled Nour off without their batons. One brown guard jammed his thumb under Nour's jaw, and Nour let go, his eyes glittering with tears.

The blonde guard would not stop yowling.

Get me to Medical, I need an airlift!

Let me see, the brown guard said, kneeling.

Radio it in—these fucking monkeys—you saw that, you saw it.

Yep, he said, inspecting the marks under her rolled-up pant leg. You've got some nice bruises.

Bruises? He bit me! Like a bloody dingo!

You're lucky he didn't break the skin. Want me to bite him back?

He bared his big white teeth at Nour, who shrank away.

Come on, Beth. Let's get you some ice.

Ice? Kiss my arse! I'm going to need stitches!

She limped away, swearing, on the brown guard's arm. Another guard spat at Atay. A fourth pinched Abay's rear, good and hard.

Think she's a good root for a monkey? Seeing as the kids came out all monkey—

What I think, Quentin, is that she'd be a good root for *you*.

Aw, lay off! I've got Ella at home, you know that.

Your loss.

When they had walked out of earshot, Atay fixed his black, burning eyes on Nour.

Next time, bite harder.

Yes, Atay. I will.

Abay was feverish and shivering when they got her onto her bunk. The Sri Lankan woman lifted the dividing sheet and scowled at them.

Sick, she said, pointing.

Yes, Atay said.

Bad, she said. Get guards.

No.

She gestured again at Abay, then held up her own frail son, who was three years too young to be of interest to Nour. His bright, curious gaze danced over their room.

She said: Guard. Sick.

No, Atay said. Sorry.

The sheet dropped, hiding them.

This time you bite the guard, Nour said to Firuzeh.

What did it taste like?

Egh.

She poked him, and he poked back harder. Now and then they snuck a glance over at Abay. Her presence was somehow worse than her absence. The sound she made was thin, high, and terrible.

Sleep, Atay said, stroking Abay's hair, but the sound went on and on and on.

Puffy little mountains of mosquito bites covered Abay's face and arms and feet, every inch of skin that was visible, down to her soles. Some had bubbled and wept golden pus. Some were crusted and caked with blood.

After a while, the sound guttered to syllables.

Hush, Atay said. There'll be time to talk later.

Abay said: Firuzeh.

Yes, Abay?

Twisting to reach behind her, Abay produced from the waistband of her skirt a pristine pair of white leatherette shoes. They were decorated with two pink punched flowers apiece.

Thank you, Abay.

Do . . .

A long breath, indrawn.

Do they fit?

Firuzeh laid the new shoes in her lap. She stuck a hand in each and spread out her fingers.

Yes, Abay, she said. They fit.

Good . . .

Abay turned her face away.

You should sleep, Atay said.

Firuzeh stuck out her right foot and made the old shoe's split seam talk. Her toes waggled like eels in its mouth. Yes, sleep, the shoe said. It'll all be okay.

I don't believe you, she told her shoe, and slung it off. It soared halfway across the tent, over the billowing sheet.

On the other side, the Sri Lankan boy started to cry.

That night, the monsoon rains began.

Rain palpitated the canvas roof and seeped in through a thousand holes. Nour's mattress poured a waterfall when he sat up on its edge.

I'm wet.

Firuzeh said: You donkey.

My blanket is wet.

Abay's voice floated out of the darkness like words spoken in a dream.

Omid, do you remember Istalif in the spring?

Climb down, Nour, Atay said. It's drier below.

But I don't want him! Firuzeh protested. Egh, Nour, you're wet!

That's what I told you. Now who's a donkey?

The arghawan in blossom, that bloomed through the war.

A brief, sodden struggle. Then her blanket was Nour's.

Hey, give that back!

Atay said: Firuzeh.

Nour said: Well, mine's all wet.

Purple on the hills and purple by the stream. And everyone picnicking on blankets.

Atay said: Firuzeh, stop hitting Nour.

Look! These are my hands! It's him hitting me!

I can't see. Atay sighed. Is it wrong to wish for a head-count? It's probably wrong.

Those shitheads won't come out in this stuff, Firuzeh said. They'll tick off our numbers and say that they did.

Where did you learn a word like that?

From the shitheads, Atay. That's what they say when they see us.

She said it, Nour said. She said it. Not me.

A longer sigh.

The rain dripped down.

If we all settle in, maybe some of us can sleep—

Ow!

Firuzeh said, indignant: You can't punch me and say *ow!*

Yes I can! I just did!

Idiot!

Ow!
I remember the boys selling tulips by the road.
Did I buy you a bunch? Atay asked the darkness.
No. I wished for them, but the bus never stopped.

CHAPTER TWENTY

Decisions arrived with a break in the rain.

Here and there the dusty ground had turned to ankle-deep wallows of rainwater and mud. Coming back from the ablutions block, Firuzeh stepped barefoot into one such pool, new shoes in her hand. Above her, a white bird with a scarlet thread of a tail dropped the small fish it held in its beak, which fell twisting and gleaming into the pool. A swift silver thing it was, no longer than her finger, darting in and out of the clouds of silt that Firuzeh stirred up with her feet.

She wadded up her skirt, squatted, and combed the water with her fingers. No luck. Her movements had turned the water opaque.

Fish puddle, she told herself, measuring its distance to the camp's single tree. The rows of dull tents pattering with rain were too uniform to mark her spot.

The rains, they had heard, would continue for months.

She'd put the fish in a bowl and feed it white bread. Little by little, the fish would grow.

A fish clock, she thought. Or a fish calendar. How much time since. Until. And when.

As Firuzeh approached her family's tent, the migration agent passed with quick, sticky steps. His face was fixed forward with such firmness, he almost trampled her.

Inside, Atay held a soft, sagging letter.

Firuzeh, you read this.

Nour said, The words are hard.

She took the damp page and held it against the triangle of pewtery light admitted through the tent's entrance.

We're Afghan, she said.

What? Of course we are. What kind of letter is this?

They're saying they know we are Afghan now. And Hazara. And not lying.

Did they think—?

Abay said, All liars think others are lying.

Atay said, Well. Some refugees might have lied. I could see a Pashtun lying. So this is a good letter. They know we told the truth.

Firuzeh said, They'll give us each two thousand dollars.

Two thousand dollars!

And plane tickets—

Do you hear this, Bahar!

—back to Kabul.

For a long time, no one spoke.

There were faint shouts outside. Other letters. Other slow and halting translations.

This letter says that Afghanistan is safe. It says, go home. They'll give us the money if we sign an agreement. Sign, go away, and never come back.

Two thousand dollars, Abay said, won't pay for one grave.
Bahar—

It's the truth.

Nour said, So when are we going to Australia?

Never, Firuzeh said. We'll die on this rock.

There must be *something*, Atay said. I'll speak to the agent.

Outside, in the quicksilver, possible light, men and women held letters, comparing the words.

We have failed to verify—

Consider the probability of falsification high—

Regret to inform you—

No possibility of return.

Some still had spirit enough to wail. Most were silent.

Abay shuffled out of the tent, shading her eyes with one hand. Her hair was a jumble, her scarf stained and askew. She had not left her bed in days. All over her hands and face the bites had scabbed over with dry yellow crystals.

Come, Firuzeh.

Firuzeh followed, splashing from puddle to puddle, as Abay made her way between the tents.

At least your Atay and I have you two. The Shahsevanis have nothing at all.

Nasima said she had brothers. What happened to them?

We don't know. The phone numbers don't work anymore. They haven't been able to reach them for months. And now this—Delruba will go out of her mind. Don't remind her of Nasima. Don't speak. Don't smile.

So why am I coming?

Abay's shoulders slumped. Because I'm your mother. And Atay's gone to find the agent.

When they reached the Shahsevanis' tent, which was identical to every other tent around it, Abay lifted the flap and waved Firuzeh through.

The Shahsevanis sat on opposite ends of the lower of their two bunks, facing away from each other.

Delruba said, Good morning, Bahar. I wish I had tea. Isn't that the worst? Even during the war, I had tea for my friends. Even if it was only one leaf. At least we have a chair.

Abay said, Did you get your letter?

You just missed the agent. It was strange. He was smiling. I couldn't come earlier, he said. The rain held me up. But now you know.

How odd. But these people, their jobs must make them odd. Saying *Go home and die* to us every day. So your letter: did they offer you two thousand dollars too?

Two thousand, what a fortune. Is that what your letter says?

They'll give us two thousand each to go back to Kabul.

Oh, shameless, shameless. No, I was a fool. Can you read this letter? the agent said. My daughter can translate it, I said. She won an award for her English at school. Then I remembered. The look he gave me split my heart like an apricot.

Firuzeh, come here! She can translate, Abay said.

Firuzeh, dragging foot behind foot, held out her hand for the folded letter.

Go on, Abay said. What does it say?

I have to read it in English first.

Nasima would have translated it already. She won two prizes for English at school, you know.

Firuzeh ignored this. She marked each word with her finger.

Mr. Rahmatullah Shahsevani and Mrs. Delruba Shahsevani—

I understood that, Delruba said.

We are pleased to inform you tat your apple-ications have been per-ocessed and apper-o-rooved. You have received A-S-I-O cul-earance and may enter Austeralia—

She squinted at the words she knew, then at the words she didn't.

So?

Be patient, Delruba, Agha Shahsevani said. Can't you see the girl is doing her best?

—An I-O-M agent will assist wit arrangements.

Take your time, Abay said.

I think— Firuzeh said.

Yes?

I think you are going to Australia.

Something dry and dead in Delruba's expression cracked to pieces. For the first time that Firuzeh could remember since the boat, Delruba looked around her, truly looked, as if seeing for the first time the bolted steel beds and the tent and her husband, whose hand fumbled along the bunk until it found hers.

Janam, did you hear her?

His tight, taut brows loosened into uncertainty.

I did, but does she really know? We have to ask somebody else—

Leaning on each other, uncertain and slow, they rose from their rest and walked into the world.

Abay stared at Firuzeh. They could hear Mr. Shahsevani's voice through the tent.

Hey, Abdul Hakim! Can you read English?

No, but this Iraqi, Mr. Sadiq Ali, can.

But I don't speak Arabic!

That's all right. He'll smile if you've been rejected, and cry and praise God if you've been accepted.

An anxious pause.

Alhamdulillah!

What about this letter?

Mr. Sadiq Ali, read this one!

Outside, men bellowed, stomped, and shouted; women ululated. Someone sang.

Abay arose like one in a trance and fought blindly with the tent's cloth until it gave way. Firuzeh, forgotten, slipped out after.

Wherever the good letters had fallen like stars, souls flashed forth from formerly blank faces. People danced in puddles, muddy to their waists. Kissed each other. Clasped hands. Spoke tenderly. Wept.

Not once on the long walk back to their tent did Abay remember Firuzeh.

She scuttled along in her mother's shadow, glaring at the revelers. She would spit if she spoke. Spit, scratch, and bite.

When they came within a few meters of their tent, Firuzeh grasped her skirt and ran. Her anger hissed out between her teeth. Now her mother would see her. There you are, she would say. Or, were you behind me that whole lonely time? Or, I am so sorry I forgot about you.

But Abay did not see. Abay's gaze was thousands of miles away.

Nour was kicking a plastic bottle filled with stones, water fanning up with each kick.

Abay went into their tent without a word.

Were you out here on your own? Firuzeh said.

I was playing with Khalil. But his letter came.

Was it good? Bad?

He seemed angry. But he's always angry. Firuzeh, what does *motherfucker* mean?

That means his letter wasn't good.

But our letter wasn't any good either.

Probably the same as his.

So why is Khalil so upset? We're stuck here together.

Maybe he doesn't like you as much as you think. Maybe you smell so bad he can't wait to leave Nauru. And now he has to stay here and smell you. For the rest of his life.

Too bad. You're also stuck smelling me.

That's what you think.

She gave the plastic bottle a small kick of her own.

Should we be upset? Should I say motherfucker too?

Firuzeh sighed. Don't say motherfucker, Nour.

Will Abay get mad?

Whole oceans of mad. She won't let you play with Khalil again.

Then I'll say I learned the word from you.

Then I'll punch you so hard you forget all your English.

Just joking, Firuzeh.

I was just joking too.

Raindrops fat as quail eggs plunked into their hair and plucked points out of puddles. Nour shrieked. Firuzeh laughed. They ran inside.

CHAPTER TWENTY-ONE

There was nothing, Atay said, that the agent could do.

Think of your family, the agent had told him.

I *am* thinking of my family, Atay had roared.

Atay said: I hope the Tajik translated what I said. That all of them are heartless, cowardly men.

You mean they are motherfuckers, Nour volunteered.

Atay blinked, then took a deep, slow breath.

I see you've been learning English, Nour. That will be useful in Australia. But while we are here, confine your cursing to Dari.

But Khalil—

—is learning the wrong things. He'll be beaten someday, like Mansour was. I don't want that to happen to you. Your mother—

They all looked at Abay, sprawled facedown on her bunk, her tired face hidden under a thinning sweep of hair.

Atay added: And if it happened, I'd hit you a few times too. So that you'd know better.

When will they let us go to Australia? Firuzeh says Nasima's parents are going.

Maybe in a few months. We have to be patient.

Because if it's never, like the letter says, we could go back to Kabul. Nour bumped his head against Atay's. *I* wouldn't mind.

These are adult matters. You don't understand.

It's Firuzeh's fault, isn't it? I want to go home. I don't care about her! I miss Abay's cooking. I miss my friends.

Quit crying, Firuzeh said. I just got this bed dry.

I miss our home, Atay. Who's living there now?

Atay said: Go out and play. I need to rest.

It's raining, Atay.

Atay screwed up his hands in his hair. Then go torture our neighbor's son. Or light a fire somewhere. Just don't kill anyone. And let Abay sleep.

Firuzeh said, Atay, you could tell us a story.

I'm fresh out, Atay said.

Then make one up.

Atay said, Firuzeh jan—this once, be quiet.

The Shahsevanis and six other refugees accepted for resettlement said their goodbyes as they stood by the green school bus that would take them to the plane to Australia. Atay had brought Firuzeh to see them off. She traced a crescent in the dust with the tip of her shoe.

Congratulations, Atay said, embracing Nasima's father. Did you find your sons?

It's the strangest thing, Rahmatullah said. They hired a solicitor with their savings. She found out where we were and started the paperwork. They'll be waiting at the airport.

Where's Bahar? Delruba said, beaming.

Not feeling well. She's lying down. She's sorry to be missing your departure.

That's too bad! Then I'll run over and say goodbye. Do we have time for that?

Please don't, Atay said, you'll miss the bus. And then the plane might leave without you. Here, let me help you load your bags.

Delruba bent down to meet Firuzeh's eyes.

You be good, she said. Like my Nasima. Be kind to your Abay. Mothers endure much more than you know.

The migration officer waved the eight refugees onto the bus. The Shahsevanis boarded along with the rest.

Atay squeezed Firuzeh's hand. They watched the bus go.

Not a word to your mother, he said.

Yes, Atay.

But news flew faster than the Simurgh. By the time Atay and Firuzeh reached their tent, visitors had already come and gone.

So fortunate, one of the women said as they passed. It must have been fate. And what a perfect person for this to happen to. Khanem Delruba is so kind and has lost so much. If any of us—

Atay winced. They found Abay sitting on the bunk, arms around her legs, black hair over her knees.

I'm sorry, Atay began. Did they—

Firuzeh said, Abay—

Fuck them, Abay said. And shit on their fathers.

The next day, Abay plodded to the kitchen to inquire after her old dishwashing job, and Atay lined up at Medical for pills.

Thus far they had not needed much medicine, since hope had done triple duty as amulet, tonic, and prophylactic. Now that the bottle had been smashed, there was no help other than nurses and pills.

Too young to visit Medical on her own—ignored by the nurses, in fact, every time she wandered close to the donga —Firuzeh imagined a pharmacological cabinet of rich dark wood that took up an entire wall. Each drawer rattled when you pulled the brass knob, shaking the blue-red-yellow-purple-white pills inside. There were pills shaped like goldfish, and pills shaped like stars, along with more boring triangles and trapezoids. Some were striped and some were speckled, and some were only one color, or three, or two. You could get pills for headaches and bad dreams and homesickness, pills for fever and forgetting and pills to not care. If you were sleepless or homeless, there was a pill for that, too.

Whatever you needed, you asked for, and they provided. That was why the line of men waiting for pills always doubled back along the path.

Wrong, Khalil said, once she expounded her thoughts. He was swinging Nour's bottle of rocks, waiting for Nour to don shirt and shoes. They have two kinds. Toothache? Fever? Panadol. Anything else, one sleeping tablet. That's everything they've got. I've been there. I know.

Then what could Atay be getting?

Panadol. Or sleeping tablets.

What did they give you?

Sleeping tablets and Panadol.

Firuzeh said: That doesn't make sense.

As if anything makes sense in this giant rat cage. Pills, Payam, Mansour. Nour, hurry up, or I'm going without you.

Nah, you won't—you've got no one but me.

What happened to Payam? Firuzeh said.

He's gone, Khalil snapped. Nour! You're taking too long!

Payam got a letter, Nour said. One of the good ones.

He hopped on one foot, tugging at his shoe.

I'm glad for him, Firuzeh said.

Good riddance! Khalil said.

Weren't you always stuck together? Like a two-for-one sale.

That's right, Nour said. Khalil, I'm ready to go.

Too late, Khalil said, flinging the bottle down. Have a beautiful—he hurled the tent flap aside—fucking day!

Khalil, I'm sorry! I was sleepy! It's so early—slow down! I'm sorry my sister is such a jerk!

Nour vanished in pursuit.

Firuzeh nudged the forgotten bottle, its plastic creased white from kicking, its sides thick and smeary with mud. The boys had put gravel and coral nubs in it, and it clattered when she rolled it over with her toe.

There was a faint noise from the far side of the tent.

The Sri Lankan boy had drawn back a corner of the sheet. He glanced at her, then at the bottle.

If you take it, she said, I'll pretend I didn't see.

The boy didn't move.

Firuzeh threw herself down on a bunk, covered her face, and let out a loud snore.

She heard a muffled giggle, then soft steps. A clacking and scraping, followed by a watchful pause. She waited until the steps had fully retreated before opening her eyes. Nour's treasure was gone.

From the other side of the sheet came a furtive rattle.

Ten minutes later, Nour whirled back into the tent like a small, wet squall.

He's so mad, Firuzeh! Was it something you said?

I think it's Payam.

Still your fault. Hey, where's our ball?

Nour peered under the bunks.

It was right here!

Maybe somebody stole it. I took a quick nap.

You're useless, Firuzeh.

She stuck out her tongue.

The dishwashing had been taken over by a Chinese woman, Abay said, whose swelling belly pressed into the steel edge of the sink. Two quarters an hour, gone like that.

We're sorry, they told her. We waited two days, then three. But look, keep on asking. People leave all the time.

You mean deportations.

Acceptances, too.

That means no more ice cream, Firuzeh told Nour.

Who wants ice cream in this weather?

Abay and Atay went together to Medical in the morning. When they came back, they lay down and closed their eyes. Then all that Firuzeh or Nour could provoke was an inarticulate mumble or a *Janam, let me rest*.

Just like Khalil, Nour said. He's on pills now too. I told him you lost our ball, and he shrugged and said, Who cares about that anymore.

Rain kept them inside, where they had to sit still. Fat bulges of water gathered on top of the tent. If you poked them, a bit of the water dripped through, but the rest poured off, and that was better than the slow drops that slid down the back of the neck. A few minutes later, they filled up again.

I want pills too, Firuzeh said. I mean what are we supposed to do?

Nour said: I'm glad you can't have them. You'd be even more boring.

What you need, Nour, is a pill for school, that will put history and science into your head. And I need a pill for annoying little brothers, who give you a headache, then a stomachache.

There's Panadol. Or sleeping tablets.

I think tomorrow I'll ask the nurse.

You'll get into trouble.

For asking?

Mm. The nurses are just fat guards, Khalil says. They're angry about being here, and they wish we were dead.

If that's what he thinks, why does he go?

He can't sleep, Nour said. Since Payam left. He cries, and then everyone in his tent yells at him. One of the Iranians hit him and bloodied his nose. But that didn't work—it scared him more. At least with the pills he can sleep during the day.

Wouldn't it be a better story if there weren't any pills?

What do you mean?

I haven't ever seen these pills, have you? Maybe every-one gets together, like for a party, and I don't know, it's a big secret—

That's because you have to take the pill right there. They give you one cup with the pill in it and one cup with water. And they watch to make sure the pill goes all the way down, so you can't save them up and swallow a bunch in one go.

Khalil told you that?

Yeah. Khalil knows lots of things. He says someone tried it a few weeks ago. They weren't checking cheeks and lips yet, so he hid one pill at a time. They took him to the hospital and emptied him out.

Maybe he thought they were pills for flying. I'd take a whole bottle if they made me fly.

Me too, but I'd only take one at a time.

That's no good. What'll you do when they run out and you're flying? You'd drop and splat into wet red gobs. What you want is to fly all the way to Australia, catch hold of a tree, and hang on. Until the flying wears off. Then you climb down.

Where would you go?

I'd walk, I guess. Walk and walk and walk and walk. No fences. No guards. Maybe walk into a school and sit down. I don't know.

That's dumb. You should find the biggest candy store, stuff all your pockets, and run away.

They'd catch you and beat you.

Not if you saved one flying pill.

You'd be dropping a rainbow trail of sweets. They'd catch you.

Maybe you. They'd never catch me.

For a long time, they listened to the sound of the rain. Five days of it left an itching in the limbs—to run, to jump, to cartwheel, or to scream. But Atay and Abay lay half asleep, the paths outside were melting to mud, and they had no dry clothes except for what they were wearing. Penned up like that, with nothing to do, you turned and bit each other instead.

They were saved by the telltale chatter of gravel.

Thief! Nour cried, scrambling down from his bunk. I'll pull all your hair out! Come out here! I will!

He paced like a lion on their side of the sheet.

Give me back my ball!

The sheet twitched. Then the rock-filled bottle flew into the cloth from the other side, striking Nour in the stomach.

Nour abruptly sat down in a puddle.

Firuzeh laughed and could not stop. She clapped her hands over her mouth to hold it in. But out it came, relentless as rain, until the tent was full of laughter and she was breathless and drowning.

Is that you, Firuzeh?

Yes, Abay.

Please stop laughing, I'm tired and need to rest.

CHAPTER TWENTY-TWO

The mess tent at lunchtime had been depleted both by case resolutions and by detainees skipping meals. The ones who remained sat separately in silence. They ate without tasting, although there was little to taste. Food fell from their open mouths. What thin life the rains left them, the pills had drained.

Here and there was a man who hadn't started that regimen, alive in a way the others were not. Their faces flashed and sparked. They ate ravenously. They banged their fists against the plastic tables and damned the food, the guards, and each other. The things they would do to the guards! and their cars! and their mothers, and then the graves of their fathers!

But one by one even those coals guttered out. It proved easier, in the end, to swallow a pill.

Another boat arrived, and the mess hall grew crowded again. The arrivals carried some news of interest, about this dictator and that war, but nothing about Abay's or Atay's families.

The living mixed with the dead and looked askance.

Nour made himself another rock bottle, but Khalil was no longer interested. Besides Khalil, no one Nour's age was left. Only a couple of children, all very young, had come in on the most recent ship.

Even when Firuzeh and Nour swung from the bars on the bunks, metal squeaking and clanging, Atay rarely noticed them.

It's like you're a ghost, Nasima said. And no one can see or hear you.

The girl stood by the bunk in the dim deep night, her arms braceleted with fish scales and shipwrecked gold.

Firuzeh said, Your parents—

I know.

I thought maybe you had left as well.

I promised, didn't I?

You did.

Here I am. A dead girl talking to a dying one. What fun. Nasima scratched one barnacled ear. It's just us awake right now. Us and the nightmares. They go hunting at this hour.

Hunting?

They eat stories. That's what they're made of. Now sleep, Nasima said, and kissed Firuzeh's cheek, her lips as slickly soft as kelp.

Abay tried, now and then. It was worse than not trying.

Once there was a woodcutter. And he had a . . . daughter? And they lived, they lived . . . I don't remember. A snake in the kindling. Mount Qaf. The peris.

Atay didn't try.

They're lost in a fog, Firuzeh said to Nour. So deep they

can't see the way out. Or each other. Or maybe it's a magic spell. And we're all trapped here until it breaks.

Nour said: How do we break the spell?

I don't know. I don't know any magic words. We could look for a witch.

What do witches look like?

They write amulets out of dirty old books. So I guess they'd be squinty with ink on their hands.

I think the nurses are witches.

If they are, they're not going to help us, genius. It'll have to be one of the detainees. But if I was a witch, and they put me in here, I'd have gotten out ages and ages ago.

I wish Atay or Abay would tell us a story.

Firuzeh said: I'm telling you a story!

Your story is no good. It sucks.

I could tell you a story that Atay told us. Listen: The mullah's son came to him with a big smile. Baba, Baba, I dreamed that you gave me a dollar! The mullah pinched his chin and said, You've been a good boy, so I won't ask for it back!

Ha. Ha. That story was dumb when Atay told it.

You're lucky Atay's sleeping.

Atay's always asleep. Anyway, Firuzeh, I need to pee.

Then go pee. I'm not stopping you.

You have to come with me.

You've gone on your own.

Remember what Abay said about sisters.

I'm not going, Nour.

Fine, then I'll pee here.

All right! Firuzeh slithered off the bunk. Let's go, you spoiled little prince.

The pools of water between tents gleamed shifting silver,

smooth as fresh car panels until Nour jumped through. Firuzeh stomped after him, grumbling.

It was drier around the ablutions block, though the reek of waste curdled the yellow air. Muddy footprints streaked the entrances. Clouds of black flies hummed and swirled.

Be fast, Firuzeh said, crumpling her shirt over her nose.

Yeah, yeah. Nour half skipped, half ran inside.

Stupid Nour. Stupid her. She should have woken Abay. Firuzeh held her breath, counting. Would Nour ever come out, or would she turn plum colors and faint?

He was taking forever. Almost certainly on purpose. Firuzeh took another breath of foulness and resolved to hide his shoes during the night.

Somewhere inside the ablutions block, glass broke with a high chime.

Nour, she said. Nour?

Firuzeh moved toward the entrance of the men's side of the block.

Nour shot out, crashing into her knees.

Khalil, he said, Khalil's in there—

So?

He's eating, he broke—

Nour, talk sense.

He didn't know I was, he had a rock—

Breathe.

The mirror, Firuzeh—he's eating the glass.

She left him shuddering there and ran toward the center of camp, arms and legs flying, until her lungs felt full of knives. Guards narrowed their eyes and muttered into radios.

Firuzeh burst upon a knot of men parsing an old newspaper.

Agha Hassani, Agha Nobody, Mansour, please, it's Khalil—

What's wrong with Khalil?

—in the ablutions block, come see—

Led by Mansour, they set off at a jog.

Faster, she pleaded, winded, stumbling after. Go faster, please.

Mr. Hassani puffed in apology over his shoulder: We can't let the guards see grown men running. They'd be over us like ticks on a sheep.

The three men had disappeared into the block by the time Firuzeh, gasping, bent over beside Nour.

Go back to the tent, she said.

I still have to pee.

Then go in the women's side. No one will mind.

Nour ducked inside.

While Firuzeh waited, a guard strode up to her. What's all the trouble?

No trouble, sir. No trouble for you.

I saw detainees running. Where did they go?

The toilet, sir. They'll be right back.

Will they now? He spoke to his radio. It sputtered in reply.

Firuzeh edged toward the men's entrance.

The guard said: Stop there.

Another guard joined him. They conferred. Then, unclipping their batons, they marched into the block.

Unnoticed, Firuzeh poked her head in.

On the far side of the ablutions block, Khalil crouched over a sink. The mirror over the sink was shattered at its center, leaving a void in the shape of a star. Light glittered in Khalil's teeth and in the gaps of his fists. Mansour, murmuring, extended his hand.

A guard said: Don't move.

Mr. Hassani said, Khalil, listen, your mother—

Mr. Nobody said, This isn't the way out.

Blood ran from the boy's mouth and pooled on the floor.

The first guard said, What's this rort, eh? He grabbed Mr. Hassani. Is all this some shithead trick?

Khalil pressed a fist to his mouth. Tried to swallow.

I need backup and Medical, the second guard said into his radio.

Your parents, Mansour said, didn't send you for this.

Knuckle by knuckle, Khalil opened his hands. Diamonds and rubies fell glinting like rain. There were cuts on his palms and his lips and his face.

Jesus, the first guard said. Boy, come with me.

Be gentle, Mr. Nobody said. His parents aren't here.

Don't tell me my business. I said, boy, come here.

The second guard said, Easy, Quentin, it's two against four.

Hands descended roughly on Firuzeh's shoulders, and she was yanked back.

You. Out of the way.

Four guards pushed past her.

Nour was waiting for her by the corner.

What are they doing? he said. What are they doing with Khalil?

She took his wet hand.

We're going now.

CHAPTER TWENTY-THREE

Atay, when she told him, said only: I see.

Abay stroked Nour's cheek, which was sticky with tears. Poor Khalil. Poor Nour.

The next day, Firuzeh went looking for news. The one man smoking under the tree grinned when she mentioned the names.

You want Mr. Hassani? He cupped his mouth. Ai, Hassani, a girl is asking for you!

From a nearby tent, cursing and crashing about. Then Mr. Hassani appeared, breathless, shoelaces undone. The other man chuckled and stubbed out his cigarette, then sauntered into the same tent.

Oh, it's you, Mr. Hassani said, stooping to tie his shoes. Omid's daughter. What do you need?

Where's Khalil?

He's been flown to the mainland. To a hospital, I hope.

He brushed dust from his collar and neatened his clothes.

Did the guards hurt you?

Not badly. They figured it out. People here—

He glanced down at her.

This isn't the first time. That this. Ah. Khalil got creative; you have to be to—anyhow. They took out the mirrors and swept up the glass. Not even a screw left. So no one else will.

Will Khalil come back?

That's up to God. I hope he doesn't. This place was bad for him.

He paused.

If that's all—

Thank you, Mr. Hassani.

He hurried off. Firuzeh sat under the tree to think. After a while, the first man slunk out of the tent, smirked at Firuzeh, and slipped away.

Not long after his departure, a woman came out of the same tent. She appeared to be younger than Abay but older than Mansour, and she fumbled cigarette and lighter twice before the flame caught. Leaning against the tree, she smoked in gray sighs.

Presently Firuzeh said, Are you a witch?

The woman coughed. Do I look like a witch?

I've never met one. I don't know. But people come to you. People would come to a witch.

If I were a witch, would I be here? But what do you want? Fortune-telling? A curse on a particular guard?

A cure, Firuzeh said. And a cure for a cure.

Sorry?

Australia said we can't come in. Now Abay and Atay take pills and sleep all day. They used to tell stories and yell at us.

Hm, the witch said, and leaned back and smoked.

Firuzeh said: Do you know the story of Bibinegar? With the snake husband and the demon wife?

Can't say that I do. And if I did, I'd mess it up, and then we'd both feel bad.

She stood, Firuzeh sat, and the whole world steamed. A pebble-brown lizard ran up the trunk of the tree. Cigarette smoke ribboned up into the branches.

Your parents are sleeping? the woman said.

Or lying still. It's hard to tell. Firuzeh mashed a cigarette stump under her shoe. Why do they do that? When I'm right here?

Sleeping is an easier way to wait.

For what?

I don't know. What do we all wait for, here?

Being let into Australia. Or being made to leave.

No, see, both of those options have come and gone. But here we are, still waiting. All of us had something to wait for, and that kept us going. Now we don't. Now the minutes of our lives are wasted. Time scrapes our nerves. It hurts. How it hurts.

Is that why you smoke?

Yes.

Smoking's very expensive.

Did your father say that?

He did. Atay doesn't smoke here, but he used to, a little. Never too much—he worked around cars.

I have ways, the woman said, of paying for them.

Are you rich?

What a question. She glanced sideways and laughed. What is rich? Who is rich?

Australians are.

Oh, you think like a migrant. Be big-souled, like me. When a guest visits your house, what does your mother do?

Pour him tea and set out nuts and white raisins. But that was in Kabul. We don't have those things here.

But. Even if you had nothing, she'd serve him some tea.

Yes.

Now we come to Australia. Knock knock. Let us in. Do they treat us like guests? Or throw us in prison? Australians are poor, girl. Your mother is rich.

So what does that make you?

Rich, pretty, and wise.

Raindrops plopped on the leaves of the tamanu tree.

There we go, the woman said. Do you want to come inside? I'm Zahra, by the way. Call me Khala if you're shy.

Firuzeh.

Come in, please.

Zahra's tent was not much different from the rest, but only half the bunks appeared to be occupied. A heavy sweat smell lingered in the nose, the same smell that was everywhere when the taps ran dry. Then, wonder of wonders, Zahra produced a kettle so dented it might have served as a helmet for a battle or two.

So, Zahra said. Can I offer you tea?

She had more than tea; she had Capelle's biscuits, two cans of cola, a whole stash of mismatched cigarettes, and half a large bag of crisps.

Firuzeh opened and closed her mouth.

Some of the guards like me, Zahra said, her voice dry. Go on, have a biscuit.

Abay would kill me.

You'd be doing me a favor. Sugar gives me zits.

Firuzeh tore open the double packet, then forced herself to eat each biscuit crumb by crumb.

You should take some with you.

My parents—

Are asleep. No, it's not proper manners, but what's proper about any of this?

The tent flap rustled. A man cleared his throat.

Excuse me, Zahra said, and went to the flap.

Firuzeh licked the sugar that dusted her fingers.

—no, I can't. Yes, I told you, but I have a guest—

With her tongue, Firuzeh collected the crumbs at the bottom of the wrapper.

—back in half an hour. Yes, I'll be here—

Zahra returned and poured them both tea, moving the bag from cup to cup until the water in both was brown.

You really are rich, Firuzeh said.

Most people here don't have much money. Not even the Nauruans, but especially not us. When there's no money, some things are almost as good. Cigarettes, for example. Very stable in value. One cigarette equals two biscuits or four small packets of crisps. Sometimes the biscuits change price. Here, take another. I meant it. Don't be so polite.

I'll take one for my brother, thank you, Firuzeh said.

What a good sister you are. Where's your brother?

I don't really know.

Look, the rain's let up. She gazed down at Firuzeh, her eyes softly sad. I wish I could tell you, come visit again. But don't. You don't know me and you never came here.

I'm very sorry, whatever I've done—

You haven't. You didn't. But now you should go.

Firuzeh sucked up the weak tea and set down her cup.
Thank you for the tea and biscuits, Khala Zahra.

Anytime. But not anytime. You understand.

Firuzeh was beginning to think that she did.

Nour's eyes should have bulged when Firuzeh presented the
biscuits. He had stayed curled up by Abay's arm the entire day.
But he barely looked at what Firuzeh swung under his nose.

It's biscuits, Nour—biscuits! Say I'm clever and they're
yours.

I'm clever, he said.

No, say *I'm*—what's wrong?

He turned away, nosing into Abay's arm.

Firuzeh said: They took Khalil to Australia. A hospital.
He'll be fine.

Nour mumbled.

What?

I said, I don't care.

Have a biscuit, though. I brought them for you.

I don't want them.

If you're sure—

Firuzeh. Go away.

Last chance.

No.

She unwrapped the plastic and pressed the edge of a biscuit to his cheek.

Nour. It's right here. It's even got chocolate.

He pushed her hand away.

She gave up, sat down, and nibbled the biscuit. Nour was
here and not here. She had and hadn't gone somewhere. The

biscuit tasted like ash in her teeth. She folded the wrapper around the other. Nour would whine and want it, once he came back to himself. She gave him an hour.

He didn't ask.

Come here, she said finally, by the dividing sheet. The curly-haired head of their youngest neighbor poked around.

She held out the biscuit. Here, take it, she said.

The boy wrinkled his nose at her, snatched the packet, and smiled. He crunched the whole thing in a single bite. Crumbs sprayed from the packet. Firuzeh brushed them from her shirt.

Thank you, he told her in his own language; his expression was perfectly intelligible.

The sheet rippled and fell straight. Her neighbor was gone.

All night, Firuzeh slept on crumbs.

CHAPTER TWENTY-FOUR

Weeks or months or centuries later—time flowed thick as honey in the camp—a postcard arrived.

The guard called Nour's name and number at breakfast, and Nour leapt from his chair, twitching, ready to run.

But no punishment came. There was only a creased card waiting for him. One side had a crayoned kangaroo, the other some stamps and a thorny scrawl.

They moved me to Baxter. From Hell 1 to Hell 2. I am sorry, I did not think you would see. I was so sad. I am still so sad.

The postcard bore no return address.

When Firuzeh finished reading him the card, Nour knuckled his wet nose.

Khalil's a bastard.

He didn't forget you. He wrote you a card. The stamps cost money, he must have worked for them—

I said, he's a bastard.

Nour—

You don't know anything.

He snatched back the card.

You know nothing about me. Or Khalil. Or Payam. I'm just an annoying baby you have to take to the bathroom. You don't know anything, Firuzeh—you don't understand!

He turned his back on her and burst into sobs.

Okay, Firuzeh said, and left the mess tent.

Well, sure, Nasima said. I didn't pay attention to my brothers either. They were just there. Like pigeons. What I'm saying is, why try to understand Nour? What's even there to understand?

Something. Maybe. Firuzeh scratched the back of her head. Something I'm missing—

Look around us. Fence. Tent. Tent, fence. What could you possibly be missing?

I don't know.

Then it can't be important. Do you still have my pearl?

It's a rock.

It's a pearl. I fought a blind squid to win it for you. Almost lost my fingers.

Is it magic?

No, I fought with the squid for fun. Of course it's magic, stupid.

Then what does it do?

Helps me find you.

That's it?

As if I didn't have to wade through night-dark oceans to see you! As if you're not worlds and worlds away in your own head! Hold tight to it, and you'll always find and be found.

But it looks like a rock.

Then you're not trying.

Much later, searching for a misplaced coin, Firuzeh lifted Nour's pillow and found the postcard underneath. The weight of his head had wrinkled it. Humidity had turned it soft. She carefully put the pillow back.

CHAPTER TWENTY-FIVE

She did not know the day or month or year. Atay's hard muscles had melted like wax, and Abay rarely spoke, only sighing. The rains had stopped. So had the boats. The detainee population on Nauru diminished, as some took the offered money and went back the way they came, and others, beaming like lotto winners, flew to new lives in Auckland, Melbourne, Sydney, or Perth.

The pregnant dishwasher was deported to China, but Abay did not return to her job.

Their Sri Lankan neighbors were chosen for resettlement. The father shook hands with everyone, accepting their congratulations with a nod. The mother hugged all of them, kissed Firuzeh and Nour, and burst into tears. Their boy said nothing, but smiled and smiled.

The tent was quieter once they had gone.

The heart hurt then like an orphaned thing. Silences built up, spar by spar, until they each floated on an island of unspoken words, whole seas of thoughts dividing them. Always, a dark shape hung on the horizon—and that was the option of return.

It was late morning and humid, the sun high. Abay and Atay had returned from the nurse's station and the daily sacramental swallowing of pills.

Outside their tent, the migration agent called their names. He tripped over the unfamiliar syllables.

Omid and Bahar Daizangi, are you home? May I come in?

Atay stirred. Abay murmured. Firuzeh jumped from her bunk and lifted the flap, and the sun boiled in.

Oh. Hello. Little girl, are your parents at home?

She backed away, still holding the flap. The agent came in.

Who is this? Nour said. Are we in trouble?

Firuzeh said: I don't know.

There you are. Hope you'll pardon my intrusion. We try to get the news out as fast as we can.

He coughed and produced a starch-white letter.

Mr. Omid Daizangi and Mrs. Bahar Daizangi, the Federal Government of Australia is pleased to inform you that on appeal, your prior denial of status has been reversed—

Atay shook his head, uncomprehending.

Abay pulled her blanket up over her face.

The agent stopped. Should I come back with a translator?

Atay said: Firuzeh—

We're going to Australia.

Nour peered over the edge of his bunk.

Stiffly, Atay unfolded himself, stood up, and grasped the agent's unready hand. Sir—

Abay tossed her scarf back over her hair and fixed it with two pins.

Firuzeh slipped out of the tent.

The world was one lustrous, unbearable gleam. She waited, waves breaking in her breath, until the sharp glitter dropped from her eyes. Here were the camp's old tents and fences, the same as they had been an hour before, yet somehow subtly changed. If she filled up her lungs and exhaled, canvas and poles and ropes would go flying. If she put out her hand, the fences would quiver and bend. Nothing caught at her; nothing tied her down. She felt she could run and run without stopping, down the glinting steel road the sun laid on the sea, running until she reached Australia.

The agent stepped smiling out of their tent, thrust his hands in his pockets, and went on his way.

Funny, Atay said, as Firuzeh rejoined them. He laid his heavy hand lightly on Firuzeh's hair. I'm still tired. I expected to be more—well, less tired.

You'll feel better tomorrow, Abay said.

But we have so much to decide! Where we'll go, how we'll live—

We'll decide all that tomorrow, Abay said. For now—oh, look at us. Let's see if the showers have any water. Please, Firuzeh, don't make that face. I can't remember the last time either of you got a good scrub.

Indonesia, Nour muttered.

That thunderstorm.

Then we must have whole continents caked onto us. Grab your things now, let's go.

I'll stay here, Atay said, and watch the tent.

Oh no you don't, Omid. You stink worst of all.

So, you're leaving, Nasima said to her.

Oh yes. As soon as we can, or sooner. Nour says, fuck all these motherfuckers. Fuck our detainee numbers. Fuck these fences. That's how I feel too.

The moon was a slender yellow boat rowing through a drift of cloud. Firuzeh had lain awake for hours, waiting for Nasima to call her name.

What will you do? she said to the dead girl.

I told you. Wherever you go, I'll go with you. We'll be sisters. We'll be best friends, you and me. It's not like you have anybody else.

What if—

What if what?

Nothing.

You'll need me, Firuzeh. Wait and see.

They were both quiet then. The whispering of the distant sea hung like a bright diamond in each of their ears.

I hate this place, Firuzeh said. I won't miss it at all.

That sounds about right.

But tonight—it's almost beautiful.

Moonlight washed the gnawed coral pinnacles, frosted the skeletal phosphate cranes, and drenched the canvas tents where a hundred dreamers dreamed gray, grim, and miserable dreams. The sky was salted with stars.

Nasima said, There's something about beginnings and endings. That polishes them so smooth you can nearly see your face in them. Then you open your hands and let them go, and the current pulls you onward and away. Behind you, those stones sink down to the mud, where no one will ever find them again.

Or maybe I've gone crazy from not sleeping, Firuzeh said. That happened to one of my cousins during the war. Forty days without sleep, he was so scared, Atay said. Then he ran screaming out of his house and into the street. They shot him immediately. No one knows which side, but it doesn't matter.

Well, you're already outside your tent. If you want to scream—

Tell me what Australia will be like.

Cruel, but a different kind of cruelty. Lonely. Harder than you could ever imagine.

Are you sure? Have you been there?

I can hear my parents dreaming from a great distance. Like a few notes of a song you half remember when you hear someone humming it somewhere.

They're giving us visas called T-P-Vs. The V stands for visa. I think a T-P is a kind of home.

Nasima said: I don't remember what home means anymore.

Firuzeh said: Home is where you're safe, but sometimes it's not safe. Sometimes it's not yours, but you can shut your eyes and pretend it is. And your family is there, and you fight and kiss. There's a bar on the gates, so no one can walk in unless you invite them. And when you do invite them, you offer them tea. And home is your school and your friends and your town.

That sounds nice, Nasima said, and was silent again.

It was bright in the tent, the light lemony. Abay was packing with neat flicks and tucks: spare clothing; rupiahs, afghanis, and cents; two photos creased past recognition; the mobile, dead with water, confiscated when they arrived.

Abay said, Have you told your friends goodbye?

Don't have any, Nour said.

Firuzeh said: Friends?

You should go tell them. Later you'll wish that you did.

Abay latched the suitcase.

The bus comes in an hour, so you'll have to be quick.

Firuzeh stood under the tamanu tree and called Zahra's name, twice, then three times.

Zahra emerged, looking rumpled and badly unslept.

Hey, you. What did I tell you?

We're leaving, Firuzeh said.

Back to Kabul?

No, Melbourne. In Australia.

Isn't that lucky. When do you go?

Today. In an hour. Less, actually. I should go back.

Hang on.

Zahra vanished into her tent. Then returned, her arms full.

Okay. Hold out your skirt.

She dropped bags of crisps and popcorn into Firuzeh's skirt, stuffed chocolates in her pockets, wedged colas under her arms. As a finishing touch, she tucked a cigarette behind Firuzeh's ear. That's for your father.

Khala Zahra, this is too much!

This is a time to celebrate. And I doubt you have anything to celebrate with. Besides, you called me Khala, and you came to say goodbye.

She lit a cigarette of her own and clamped it tight between her teeth.

Don't let them break you or turn you hard. This world is a harsh place and not made for you.

Khala Zahra, you're crying.

Don't be silly. I don't cry.

Will you be okay?

Always am. Go back before you miss the bus—and don't you drop those!

They boarded their flight at Nauru's tiny airport. Although the plane was all but empty, they sat as close together as they could. Atay held Nour's hand; Abay, Firuzeh's. Firuzeh's heart beat as loud as a rabbit's. At any moment an officer might come by to tell them, so sorry, Mr. Daizangi, there's been a mistake—

Where in the world did you get these, Firuzeh?

A friend.

I thought you didn't have friends.

I guess I was wrong, Firuzeh said.

She unwrapped a bar of Turkish delight and held each bite in her mouth for a minute. The chocolate coated her tongue and teeth. The jelly dissolved.

The plane taxied away from the gate. Suddenly Firuzeh was compressed into her seat. Her teeth began to throb and ache. Outside the round window, Nauru shrank to a spot.

Beginnings and endings sank like stones through the mind.

Several hours later, they fell out of the blue and shining sky, down and down, into autumn, and Melbourne, and a blood-thickening cold.

PART TWO

CHAPTER ONE

In Melbourne you could find anything you wanted, if you had the money and knew where to look. On the weekends when Atay had to meet with a caseworker, the entire family took the train into town. From their crane-littered suburb it was a short ride. Firuzeh stood and swayed, staring, as grey eucalyptus, mica towers, and concrete flats rushed past.

Flinders Street Station, glazed gold on the inside, echoed like an enormous shell. Metal trams screeched and clanged in the street. Traffic signals clicked and flittered: walk, walk, wait. Steam curled and coiled in alleyways. Graffiti glistened and glowed on walls.

Every time they passed the State Library Victoria, Atay pointed to the statue in front.

It's Rostam slaying the dragon! And Rakhsh with him! How did these Australians know?

Abay kept a tight grip on Nour's slight shoulder. Otherwise he hurled himself at every shop window rainbowed with candy, fussing until Atay scooped him up or he was permitted a cheekful of lollies.

Disgraceful, Abay sighed. You weren't like this when we lived in Kabul. What happened, Nour?

Nour shrugged and chewed.

Firuzeh would sooner have died of shame than mash her face into shop windows like Nour. Her teachers wrote notes about her polite shyness that Abay and Atay could not translate.

What does this say? Atay asked, holding one up.

It says I am the best possible daughter, that my homework is without equal in my class, and you should thank God for blessing our family with me.

Atay snorted. Very funny. What does it really say?

That I'm polite and very quiet.

Even funnier. You?

Can't help it, she said. I was raised that way.

But the Firuzeh who slapped one palm on her desk and shot her other hand high into the air, the Firuzeh fizzing with answers and fishing for praise, had been left in a locked-up, empty house on a dusty street in a past Kabul.

The other students twittered and chirped, words flickering and flashing too quickly to catch. Firuzeh laughed slowly and laughed last, under impatient, silent stares, on the rare occasions when she grasped the joke. She never found herself on the right page of the book, much less the right paragraph, and she blushed and sank low when her teachers called her name. It did not matter which class she sat in; maths, English, or science, it was all the same. She was unprepared, ignorant, behind.

Morning recess was her only reprieve. The whole primary school spilled into the yard, where chalk faces and game squares whitened the asphalt. Gaggles of children, Nour among them, shouted *What time is it, Mister Wolf,* then scattered with shrieks.

Nour never had trouble making friends.

Firuzeh, meanwhile, stood in a shady corner and watched, wishing she were young enough to join in. It was nevertheless a relief to be briefly invisible, and not pinned like an insect by the teacher's finger.

This lasted six weeks, give or take. Then a Greek girl from maths class, Mia, walked up to Firuzeh and stuck out a hand. Two other girls trailed her, one pimpled, one peeved.

Gulalai here says you're a queue jumper. Is that true? Did you come here in a boat? What was that like? Mia swung her head, and her rhinestone earrings flashed. Could you shower? Did it stink? Did anyone drown?

This is Gulalai, the sugar-spotted girl said, patting the third girl's shoulder. In case you wanted to punch her. I'm Shirin. Gulalai's gullible, so please excuse her.

Am not.

She repeats whatever's blabbed on TV. Welcome to Australia, I guess.

You people, Gulalai said, didn't wait your turn. Your visas should have gone to my uncle and aunt. Her face was flushed.

Gul, Dad calls the Immigration Minister a right bastard. A lot of what he says isn't true.

That's a pollie for you, Mia said with a shrug.

Shirin said: So we figured—I figured—you didn't have any friends.

Mia said, beaming: We decided to let you join us for now.

Gulalai said, I didn't.

Shut up, Gulalai.

Mia said, You don't have to listen to her.

Firuzeh said, Actually, I have a friend.

Where is she? Shirin said, spinning to scan the schoolyard.

Not—not here. Her family's gone to a city called Perth.

Mia said, That's so far west you fall off the continent.

Shirin said, She doesn't count.

Gulalai said, squinting, I think you're lying. I think she doesn't exist.

In the mazy April sunlight, it was possible to believe her. Nauru was thousands of miles away, nothing left of it but a pebble in Firuzeh's pocket. Perhaps even now Nasima sat on a throne of foam and counted herds of sea serpents and cuttle-fish, the memory of Firuzeh washed blank and smooth, like writing on intertidal sand. Perhaps Firuzeh had moved into a simpler world, where dead girls stayed dead and living girls played, innocent of mortar, rifle, and mine.

Shirin said: We all know about *your* imaginary friends, Gul.

Tell Froozay, Mia said. It's Froozay, right? That's what Mrs Pierce calls you . . .

Or not simpler, but different.

Gulalai said, I don't know what you're talking about.

Oh, Gul, come on. You used to tell us all about them. How you'd talk for hours while bullets zapped your house. They'd hide with you and say when to get up. When to stay down. Then they'd tell you stories—

Gulalai's face had grown blotchy and dark. I didn't, Shirin. I never said that. Stop.

Can't take what you dish, Mia said, clicking her tongue. Don't cry now. You wouldn't feel so bad if you weren't such a cunt to Froozay here.

It's not fair, Gulalai said. Five minutes and you've gone and ruined everything. Just like a queue jumper. Boat trash. Bitch.

Firuzeh said in Dari, I spit on your mother.

Shirin laughed and clapped her hands.

Gulalai said, You watch your back.

I don't have to, Firuzeh said. I have friends.

That's what you think. You'll see. Some friends.

Gulalai spun around and swept inside.

Mia said, Now what was that about?

Our Firuzeh has guts.

That's good. We need guts. Guts and brains.

Shirin said, Gulalai can be fun, but she's two sandwiches short of a picnic. You seem much sharper than her. Are you, Firuzeh?

Yes, Firuzeh said. Would have said the same if the given quality had been *reptilian, feckless,* or *weak.* Yes to anything; she'd be all of these. Already the weeks of her lonely watch were dimming in her memory. Already new courage flowed molten in her veins. She could climb mountains now. Crush automobiles.

For a moment she wondered if Gulalai's unseen friends were drowned, burned, shot—had names—if they, like Nasima, had once lived and breathed.

And then the bell rang, and the thought was lost to her.

CHAPTER TWO

Every day, Atay searched for work. He rode buses on routes that spiralled farther and farther from home, watching for garages. When he spotted a likely prospect through the window, he pulled the cord and got off at the next stop. If the owners were Afghan or Iranian, he was invited in for a cup of tea.

By and by, the ordinary, courteous questions always looped around to his visa status.

Ah, TPV, now that is hard—

We already have all the men we need—

Someone will want you, I'm sure of it.

When the owners were white, there was no tea, which was a blessing on his poor abused bladder, he said. Their questions, too, were different.

Do you have your own tools?

You speak English, mate? English? You—speak?

Sorry, you seem like a good bloke, but we can't use you here.

And at each place Atay would nod his thanks and leave, desperately wishing to use the bathroom but too embarrassed to ask. He slipped into fast food joints instead.

He drank, he told Abay, whole oceans of tea.

But no job, she said.

But no job.

In the evening, after dinner was cleared off from the flowered plastic dastarkhan, Abay and Atay had Firuzeh sit and review her language homework with them. At these times, Nour smartly disappeared.

Her materials were deadly dull. The girl Anna had a blue face. No one knew why. She might be a dead girl, Firuzeh suggested. Her teacher had raised her eyebrows at this. The lizard was named English, and that too went unexplained.

We go thorough terrees—

Through, Atay.

No, through is, I through ti ball.

That's *throw*.

Yes, yes, Abay said. Anna go throw terrees to estreet.

Firuzeh mangled her pencil with her teeth.

In Kabul, Atay knew the names of everyone and everything, which streets were safest each day and why, how many Pine cigarettes each checkpoint required, and who to call when a bomb went off. Abay knew the shifting prices of tomatoes, eggs, flour, salt, and vinegar as if she smelled them in the morning on the wind, and how to sting village dogs on the snout with stones and climb over old walls in heavy skirts.

Here they expected Firuzeh to teach them letters.

The world had bruised and gone soft, and now impossible things teemed and wormed out of it.

Here were monsters, the most monstrous being daily life.

I can't do this, Firuzeh said.

I know it's hard, janam, but we need you to.

Can't you watch TV?

We have to buy a TV first.

Atay said: You're our daughter. We have nobody else.

Abay said: I could tell you a story afterward—

I don't want, Firuzeh said, your dumb old stories. You keep forgetting the middle parts.

It's true, Abay said. There are white holes in parts of my stories. I don't know what happened to my mind.

Atay said: I don't know what happened to this girl. Did she use to speak to her parents like that?

The pencil wood was mealy upon her tongue. The graphite tip had its own smooth taste, like metal and ink and unwritten things.

I can't teach you. I'm not good enough. Or maybe you're unteachable. I want to be normal, Atay-o-Abay. Normal girls don't teach their parents English. Normal girls go to the shopping centre. Or movies.

Abay said: We're not normal anything, Firuzeh. Not yet.

We should be. I want to be.

Atay said: It's no use talking to her. Aren't you ashamed, Firuzeh? Acting like this at your age?

All right, Firuzeh said, her face and chest aflame. Let's try again. Where should Anna go to find English?

Throw terrees to estreet—

Wrong, she said. Wrong, wrong, and wrong.

In her restless hands, the pencil snapped.

The breezeblock flat assigned to them was cold and reeked of paint, and the cheap carpet scuffed the soles of their feet, but it was theirs for now, theirs and theirs alone. Firuzeh was queen of half a room, whose small, high window overlooked a hedge. Black-and-white magpies sometimes sang songs outside that were different from the songs of magpies in Kabul.

The other half of the room was Nour's. Two mattresses occupied most of the floor.

Firuzeh had just unslung her bag when the doorbell shrilled its acid note. Atay was on a bus somewhere, hunting for work in the city suburbs, and Nour had gone to the park with his soccer-mad friends. Abay, caught in the middle of her ceaseless scrubbing, rolled down her sleeves and dried her hands. Firuzeh climbed onto the kitchen counter and craned her neck to peer outside.

The window was small and badly placed. She saw an edge of brown sleeve and a puff of pale hair.

The door groaned as Abay opened it.

Hello! Mrs Daizangi?

Yes. Hello. How are you?

I'm Sister Margaret. I phoned last Tuesday—

Ah, yes. Come in?

—from St Kilda Sanctuary. You're a new placement, so we thought we'd check in. What a beautiful girl.

Her tiny gold crucifix spun on its chain.

What's your name, possum?

Firuzeh, her coat—

The brown coat was heavy and dusted with white hairs. The satin lining smelled of wet dog and lavender. Firuzeh draped it over the back of a folding chair, then caught chair and coat as they toppled over.

I'm sorry I couldn't come earlier. We had a couple of court cases, a medical crisis—

The sister wore a teal cardigan and loafers with tassels. Her pastry-coloured hair had gone halfway to grey. She turned a watch around and around her wrist.

It's lovely to meet you, anyway. Oh, thank you, this smells wonderful. Is that cardamom?

Opening her leather bag, she withdrew a sheaf of papers.

Abay winced.

Has anyone walked you through Centrelink entitlements? Sometimes they do, sometimes they don't.

Yes okay. Abay arranged the remnants of a package of biscuits on a flowered plate. Please. For you. This is.

Thank you, that's very kind of you.

Firuzeh watched the stranger eat one of the last four biscuits left in the flat. She sucked her teeth, mouth sour with longing. The sister's fingers pricked points in the air, describing this and that implausible thing: food banks, job assistance, meal programmes, advocates. Another biscuit disappeared.

Quick, Firuzeh, more tea, Abay said. We can't let her think she's in a sloppy home.

Firuzeh took the fifty-cent thermos and mug and refilled the kettle on the range. When the water was ready, she fetched tea, cardamom pods, sugar, looked twice at the sugar, then shook something else into her palm, tipped it into the mug, and stirred it thoroughly.

One biscuit was left when she returned with both the sister's steaming mug and the full thermos of tea.

Thank you, possum. I was telling your mother about after-school lessons for you, and about some of the volunteer English tutors I know . . .

She worried the watch in its silver circle around her dry and bony wrist. Steam furled from her tea.

Wouldn't that be splendid, though. A tutor coming to teach your parents. She says you've been doing a tremendous job, but I'll bet you're exhausted. How old are you?

Ten.

Sister Margaret lifted the mug and sipped. A strange expression came over her face.

All okay? Abay said, tuned like a foil-wrapped antenna to the slightest static in her mehman's mood. Firuzeh's heart skipped a wild beat.

I could have sworn—

Sister Margaret's eyes fixed on Firuzeh, suddenly sharp. Her sparse brows twitched.

Excuse me, Mrs Daizangi, I get foggy sometimes. All these memories, you know. Sometimes one floats up, and I float away. Now what was I saying? Ah, yes. English tutors—

The level of tea in the mug held steady. The last chocolate biscuit remained on the plate.

At last Sister Margaret stood, straightened her papers, and tucked them away.

Thank you for having me.

Please, dinner. Soon my husband is coming—

Maybe another afternoon. I have some other visits to make. It was lovely to meet you, Mrs Daizangi.

Bahar.

Then call me Margaret. Good to meet you, Miss Firuzeh.

Abay stirred in protest. No, leave that—

I must insist.

Sister Margaret emptied the mug of tea down the drain, then set the mug in the sink. At a glance from Abay, Firuzeh shot forward to collect their guest's shoes and wrestle the dog-haired coat off the chair it hung on.

Then the sister was gone. The last chocolate biscuit vanished into Firuzeh's mouth, followed by the crumbs and a smear of chocolate left on the plate.

Abay poured herself a cup of tea.

What a generous woman. It helps to know there are people like that. But did you see the hair all over her coat! And that moment when she was drinking her tea. Surely she's not that old. Surely her mind's sound . . .

Firuzeh, her mouth full, did not disagree. Then a thoughtful look came over Abay's face. She went to the sink, ran her finger around the inside of the mug, and put that fingertip into her mouth.

Startled frogs did not leap faster into streams. Firuzeh made it most of the way to her bedroom, her hand reaching for the doorknob, before her mother's slipper ricocheted off her head.

Some time and some while passed, the days alike, the nights unpredictable. There were nights she slept deeply, remembering nothing. But other nights, after Firuzeh closed her eyes to the dimness of the room—as her legs, tingling, turned to lead, and a purer darkness descended upon her sight—

> glass
> glass
> broken glass
> > the high pointed teeth of the Hindu Kush
> > > all glass
> > > shining

Khalil

    blood
    heat
    humidity

teeth
   gnashing teeth
     teeth made of glass
       teeth stained with blood
       hands pouring blood
        trying to catch

She was running
forever running
her breath glassy and shattered and sharp in her throat
she had been running for ages and had to
         no   she could not stop

Behind her leapt a grey thing all
       GLASS TEETH
        and
            HUNGER

    the skin of dead people slipping loose from their skulls
    the streets were full of
    the roads were paved with

she stepped on loose skins slimy and wriggling
  with rot
      the faces stared at her
         the mouths opened
            wordless

she did not know them
no
she did
Khalil
Nasima
Mansour
a cousin
an aunt

she slipped—
    the glass teeth closed on her—

CHAPTER THREE

Between the four of them, they had one mobile, which went wherever Atay went. The flat also had an old white phone. Atay's voice crackled out of its handset, irate.

It's dark out. Can't you wait?

It's winter, Abay said. There's not enough time to do everything before the sun goes down. Besides, this is Australia. We've survived wars, we survived Nauru—how dangerous can one shopping trip be? We need esfand, and teacups—they have everything, this store. That's what I've heard. I'll take Firuzeh and Nour. We'll be back before dinner.

Firuzeh said: Abay, I don't want to go.

Me neither, Nour said.

I need your help to carry things. Sometimes you have to give your mother a hand. If your classmates' parents saw me struggling to carry bags of good things home to you, what would they think?

Naturally, there was no answer to that.

The trip was precisely as long and boring as Firuzeh expected. Some hours later, she, Nour, and Abay clanked and clanged to the bus stop, weighed down on all sides with purchases, from velvety rose-patterned blankets to pitchers and plates. It was cold, the shelter of little effect. Firuzeh shivered, her bags rustling. The neighbourhood was an unfamiliar one, the streetlamps few and far apart, and the gum trees cast unwelcoming shadows.

Let me see, Abay said, riffling a paper timetable. Firuzeh, come here, help me figure out what time—

A pink-faced man walked up to the stop.

It says the bus'll be here in fifteen minutes. Firuzeh flapped the timetable shut. That's a long time, Abay. It's freezing. I'm cold.

The man glowered at Abay. Burst capillaries cobwebbed his nose and cheeks. When Firuzeh looked up, he crossed his arms.

Abay felt for the sides of her scarf, smoothing it down over her neat hair. Then she gripped their hands so tightly that their fingers purpled. Though Firuzeh's eyes watered from the pain, neither she nor Nour made the slightest sound.

Abay met the man's gaze.

A minute passed.

He spat, a horking, viscous sound. The wad of mucus darkened the footpath, barely missing Abay's shoe.

Bunch of terrorists.

Abay's gaze never wavered, but her arms were steel as she pushed Firuzeh and Nour behind her. They knocked against each other. Bag crashed against bag. Abay's lay unattended at her feet, handles drooping.

No one else was on the street. Night gathered a breath and held it in.

The man said: Go home. We don't want you here.

We go home.

That's right. Go back to your godforsaken country. Arabs, towelheads, all of you. Dog piss, that's what you are. Get out.

Cars passed in perfect indifference. The pink man's meaty hands closed into fists. He took a step toward them. Nour whimpered. Abay tensed. Firuzeh's fingers felt nearly wrung off.

Then the headlights of the 901 blazed through the darkness.

As the bus squeaked and steamed to a stop, Abay heaved them aboard. Firuzeh barked her shin on a step as she climbed on. The bags were hopelessly jumbled; she and Nour tumbled them into empty seats.

On the top step, Abay swiped her card and turned.

Australia is home, Abay said.

Fuck yourself with a rock, Firuzeh said.

The bus driver said, Are you coming, sir?

The man stared at them.

No, he said at last. No, not tonight.

The bus doors shut. The 901 lurched on. Abay dragged Nour's feet off the seat, leaned against their teetering pile of bags, and put her face into her hands.

Firuzeh looked out the bus window into the night. The man stood at the kerb, staring after them, but he and the bus shelter soon shrank out of sight.

I should have been there.

I wished you were.

This is what happens when you go outside after dark—

꩜꩜꩜

Shirin laughed and Mia gasped at Firuzeh's story over lunch.

Bloody beautiful Australia, Shirin said. All the hoons, bastards, arseholes, and cunts you could want.

I can't believe— Mia said.

Shirin said, Yes you can. She had bent the tines of her plastic fork this way and that until they broke, and now she squeezed her handful of tiny spines. It happened to Gulalai's mum too. Besides, Firuzeh doesn't seem crazy to me. Does Firuzeh seem crazy to you?

Firuzeh did not touch the white pebble she kept in her pocket.

Mia pouched a bite of green apple in her cheek and gave Firuzeh a once-over.

Na-a-o-o, she said, extending the vowels. She crunched her apple and gulped. But Gulalai—

Oh, who cares about Gulalai?

CHAPTER FOUR

It's a church, Atay said, gazing at the small brick building. They had taken two buses to reach the address that Sister Margaret provided them over the phone. Your new friend sent us to a church.

Abay said: The sister said to go around the back.

Will there be boys? Nour asked.

Firuzeh said, No one knows, elbow hat!

It's hat full of elbows, idiot. And you can't *be* one. You can only be uglier than.

An alley led around the back, past parked cars to a basement door. There was a compact kitchen inside and a cork noticeboard pinned with enormous letters—RICHMOND REFUGEE COMMUNITY CENTRE—and a dozen adults on couches and folding chairs, including two in university hoodies. They glanced up at the creaking door.

Shit, Nour said quietly.

Nour, shut up.

Atay said, Hello . . .

Hi! I'm Claire, from Monash University. Can I show you around?

Indeed she could.

Meanwhile, your kids—Mrs Sorisho—?

A woman with tiny gold flowers in her ears found trays of watercolours, brushes, paper, and a cup.

You can paint with me if you want, she said. She wetted her own brush and swept out a red flower with six petals in a single stroke.

Nour chewed his lip, then accepted brush and sheet and scraped at the disc of hard black paint.

Firuzeh dipped her brush in the paper cup and painted colourless peaks and snow. From one corner to the other, she spotted and sprinkled water. Here, zigzags. There, cliffs. The paper puckered.

I'm done, Nour said, holding his painting up.

His paper was wet and completely black at the centre. At the edges, violence: shearing slashes, splatters, single brush-strokes like razor gashes.

Mrs Sorisho slid her glasses down from her hair.

Yes, yes, she said. That's it exactly.

Can I go now?

Of course. Look in the other room. I think you will see something you like.

He slipped off the couch and padded away.

Now what did you paint there?

Firuzeh said, Glass.

Hm. Yes, I see. How else to paint glass?

Firuzeh had used the same cup of water as Nour. The water had blackened from his brush, and smoke and ash swirled from his painting into hers. Broken windows in a riot, she thought. Or a mirror, streaked.

Mrs Sorisho said, Is your family new? I have not seen you here before.

We only arrived four months ago.

Welcome, welcome.

Mrs Sorisho filled her own page with flowers.

What you were saying to Nour—that's my brother—

Yes?

Is there something in his painting? It's all black—

With slow, careful motions, Mrs Sorisho rinsed her brush, dried it on a napkin, and laid it down. A thin furrow dug into her brow.

We left our three children in Iraq.

Why?

We thought it would be safer. It seems we were wrong.

But what does that have to do with the painting?

I think you will like this picture better. Here. Have some flowers. It's yours, if you want.

Mrs Sorisho had painted a walled flower garden. A rainbow above, feverish colours below. Firuzeh held the soft damp paper on her palms.

It's nice.

Thank you.

But I still don't—

Dinner's ready, Sister Margaret said. She had entered unnoticed with three covered dishes. Claire was stirring a pot on the stove.

Nour ran in.

Firuzeh, foosball! I was going to beat Mo, but they called us for dinner—

The young man behind him said, I was about to beat *you*.

They all converged upon the long laminate table. Firuzeh wound up seated between Abay and a tall, quiet man named Samuel. Ladling lentils onto her plate, he said: Eat up if you want to grow strong like me.

He had played tuba in the army band. The band played for President Isaias Afwerki. Processionals when he walked in. Recessionals when he walked out. Anything the President liked, for eight long years.

You were in the army?

Eritrean men have to serve for a year and a half.

You said eight years.

The President's maths was a little different from the arithmetic of common men.

This is Mo, Nour was saying, from Somalia—

You're not half bad, Mo said to him.

How did you get to Australia? Firuzeh said.

The whole band came. They told us the night before our flight. Otherwise people deserted in droves. I hugged my wife goodbye. She was pregnant and bigger around than me. When we got here, they locked us inside a hotel.

How did you get out?

A political demonstration. Some Australians heard that we were here. They marched outside with painted sheets. We didn't talk about it—no one talked about it—but in the middle of the night we snuggled our instruments in our beds, so it seemed we were sleeping, and jumped out of the windows.

It must have hurt.

The protesters were waiting for us. They stretched out their banners, and we landed in them. Twelve of us made it. Then lights snapped on inside the hotel. The protesters put us in their cars and argued about us, what to do and where to go. The next day they brought us to an immigration office, and we filed for asylum. Now here I am.

And your wife?

Still in Eritrea. Along with my son. I have never seen him.

Along the table one word rose up:

Someday—

Someday our children—

—here, someday.

Firuzeh, Nour said, you have to watch. I'm going to beat Mo in two of three games.

Mo said, You can referee.

Nour could barely see over the edge of the foosball table, but he twirled the black handles furiously. The ping-pong ball clattered from row to row, then dropped into Nour's goal.

I'll win the next two.

We'll see, Mo said.

Here's the ball, Firuzeh. This time you drop it in.

Last time it was you, Mo said.

So?

I'm just saying.

Firuzeh held the white ball over the centre line. The rods of plastic figurines twitched. She let go.

The ball bounced, and their first kicks flew wild.

Bit by bit, tap and stop, Mo took possession of the ball. Nour made wet spit noises and effortful grunts, running back and forth to slam and block.

Light as air, the ball darted into Nour's goal.

Mo laughed and shook Nour's hand. Play again? You said three.

Nour pouted. No. I'm better at soccer.

Soccer, then! Someday!

Mo was taller than Atay. Firuzeh stifled a laugh.

Abay came to the doorway. We're going now.

On the bus, Abay said, What a wonderful painting. Omid, didn't you promise me a garden, once?

Yes, it's pretty. That's nice, Firuzeh.

Nour said, But—

Firuzeh tweaked his ear.

Did Nour paint one?

Firuzeh said, He was busy.

I was thinking we could plant a garden in the yard.

Atay said, I don't know. There are rules about it.

But a garden, Omid.

Someday. That man we met, Ali Reza—

He seems like a decent man.

His cousin owns a garage. He'll ask about a job for me.

Nour said: I would have won. If I dropped the ball. But you mucked it up.

Did not.

Did too.

Abay said, That would be very kind. We'll have to ask him over. Ali Reza and his wife.

Firuzeh said, Make mantu, please.

No, aush, Nour said. A lot of it.

Mantu.

Aush.

We'll make both, Abay said. If Ali Reza finds Atay a job.

CHAPTER FIVE

By August, when frost glittered grey on lawns, Atay was working in Ali Reza's cousin's Richmond garage.

There was never extra money, and after Abay saw their first electricity bill, the space heater Sister Margaret had found for them stayed on for only one hour each day. But there was enough.

Gradually, the steam of Abay's meals laid down warm layers throughout the flat. Each oil-hissing or white-billowing pan turned a fraction more of *here* to *home*.

Then one day at school, in the gossiping interval between bells, when the surf of students crashed against hallways and bubblers, rolling in every direction toward their next classrooms, Shirin slapped a card into Firuzeh's hand.

Birthday party, she said. You better come.

I'll ask.

The fuchsia paper was thick and smooth. Firuzeh rubbed her thumb over the foil letters.

Know what we'll have? Ice cream cake. Fairy bread. Tim Tams. Gosh-e-fil. Ab-e-dandan. Pavlova. Lamingtons. My parents promised. The sugar high will last for days.

No wonder your name is Shirin.

Very funny. Original. I've only heard that from my dad, oh, fifty times. So you're coming, right? Oh, oops, sorry, your parents. I forgot. I hope they'll let you out of detention for some fun.

Abay, wiping her fingers and taking up the card, said: Absolutely not.

You didn't even look at it!

I don't have to. We don't know her parents. What kind of people they are.

All we're doing is eating biscuits and cake. That's what a birthday party is.

O friend, what is better? Sugar or the One who created it?

Mum!

Abay dropped the card on the counter and stirred the pot of rice.

Firuzeh, what would people *think*?

So that was that.

In the long and colourless days between the invitation and Shirin's rainbow-sprinkle party, it seemed that no girl in Year 5 could think, talk, or dream about anything else.

What are you wearing?

Purple velvet dress, silver belt, a scarf—

Hands traced neckline and necklace over the school's white and blue.

Bringing as a gift?

Six bottles of nail polish.

Strawberry lip gloss. Or passionfruit. Unless I buy both.

This beaded bag I saw at the mall—

Here she comes.

Hi Shirin!

We weren't talking about your—

Shh! Be quiet!

Queenly, round-faced, and supremely content, Shirin glided past muffled giggles of conspiracy. The whole school was in on it. Even Gulalai.

What about you, Firuzeh?

Yeah, what will you wear?

But why not? Shirin had said in surprise. Your marks are fine. I mean, not great, but—sorry, I peeked over your shoulder once. Are they very traditional? Your parents? Oh well. Maybe next year.

And Shirin whirled away.

There was a hole in Firuzeh's chest where she had been scooped out with a silver spoon. The hole was shaped like ice cream and lamingtons. Overnight, she had been severed from the communal life of the school, exiled, banished, disenfranchised; for wherever two or more girls gathered, the party was there also.

Twenty times a day, Firuzeh bit her knuckles to keep the tears in, until they were swollen, red, and bruised.

Oh, Mia said, Firuzeh's here, we should talk about something different—

We should, Shirin said. But do you think I should wear the green dress or the orange one?

None of them truly meant to be cruel: not Abay, not Mia, and not Shirin. And that only made it doubly unfair.

At night, Firuzeh punched her pillow and muttered until Nour threw his at her and said: Go to sleep!

The day of Shirin's party, Firuzeh's nerves sparked and snapped. Every class, one girl or another was reprimanded for loud whispering, or passing notes scribbled in pink glitter pen.

Please, Gulalai, Mr Early said. Why can't you be more like Firuzeh here?

Gulalai gawked, then laughed until her eyes sparkled with tears.

The last bell was a mercy.

Goodbye, Shirin sang on the school steps, goodbye, I'll see you all soon. In an hour, remember!

It was a long and windy walk home from school. Nour skipped alongside Firuzeh, noisy as a cockatoo.

He said: Jake fell out of a tree and broke his leg.

That's nice, Nour . . .

Which means he can't play sevens now. Which means they need a substitute. Which means—

Nour. I don't care. Be quiet.

Atay, Nour said over dinner, I have to. Please. Or they'll ask Aaron, and *he* runs like a goat.

How much does it cost?

The league is seven dollars.

Only seven dollars?

. . . every week. And the shirt is twenty dollars. And I need soccer boots.

In Parwan, Atay said, we played soccer barefoot.

Yes, Atay, but—

And without twenty-dollar shirts. Twenty dollars! You could live for a year on that.

But Atay, this is Australia.

Ask your mother if we can afford it.

Maman, madar jan, mum darling, Abay—

Mum darling, Firuzeh echoed, smirking.

That's a lot of money, Nour. I don't know.

I'll do all my homework and prayers for a week. Without you asking. I promise.

Atay said, Nour should be playing with other boys. Running around. It's good for him. You should hear my brother Hassan's little ones. They never stop.

Abay said, Last I checked, running and playing were free.

Nour said, It's only five weeks.

I can ask my boss for a loan. It's not that much. I'll pay him back.

Nour, can you borrow your friend Jake's shirt?

He's huge! It's like a dress on me!

You wear that dress, Atay said, and you can play in this league.

While washing up, Firuzeh broke a plate in the sink.

Go on, Abay said, break more plates. Why else do I bother buying them?

Firuzeh burst into hot and furious tears.

Abay sighed. What a reaction. Just go.

Firuzeh slunk into her room, plopped onto her mattress, and stared at the darkness in the high window. Somewhere, girls were licking frosting off their glossy pink lips, admiring their sequinned and ruffled finery, and laughing together until their sides hurt.

Once there was and once there wasn't a girl who couldn't go to a party. As a result, she turned invisible.

That sounds like a drippy girl story, Nour said.

Go away if you want. You don't have to listen.

Nour dropped his schoolbag and laid his head in his hands.

Whenever she talked, people looked around, but they didn't see her. So they stopped looking and listening. People tripped on her. It was hard for her to stay out of their way. But she could wag school whenever she wanted to, take candy from a milk bar without getting caught, eat hot pies with out paying, and sneak into cinemas.

Okay, so she was happy.

Except for the loneliness.

Who needs friends when you have all that?

She had friends, but they stopped seeing her. Like everyone else. She tried to write, but they couldn't or wouldn't see.

Friends do that, Nour said.

Her family worried until she said, I'm right here! Then they stopped worrying and forgot she was there. Talk about modesty—even her own family never saw her hair! Every now and then her mother said, Please do the dishes. If she wanted to, she did, and if she didn't want to, well, that was too bad. I didn't hear you, she could say. I wasn't nearby.

The girl decided to get a job. I could work for you, she told the police, or I could work for a thief. The commissioner said, the job is yours. She worked when she wanted to and solved many cases, because no criminals could tell if she was listening.

Then one day, she met an invisible man—

I knew it, Nour said. They got married. The End.

But he was a thief. She was guarding the most precious vault in a bank when she saw the locks trying to turn themselves. No you don't, she said. He jumped in fear, but she didn't see that. She chased him and almost caught him many times, but it's hard to catch an invisible thief. Finally she did, and they locked him up and threw a big party for her, because she was old and famous by then. They hit the stick with the drum and the drum with the stick, and they gave the criminals raw food, and the constables cooked, and I didn't get one nibble from the bottom of the pot.

Okay, Nour said grudgingly. That wasn't too bad. If you wag school, though, can I come with?

Of course not, donkey.

I'll tell Abay if you don't take me.

When did I ever say I would skip class?

In your story.

Forget it.

Remember, I'll tell.

How are you still such a pain in the arse?

Practice, Nour said with a giant grin.

Lugging her schoolbag and lagging behind Nour, Firuzeh glared vinegar and sour milk at the rust-freckled car parked in front of their flat. Visitors meant salaams and doroods to everyone, no eating until the guests were done, and a mountain of dishes to wash before dinner.

But there were no strangers taking tea in the flat.

That car? Abay glanced out distractedly. It was the colour of eggplant and equally ugly. Atay bought it.

He what?

Abay was filling a bucket at the sink, a tall mop leaning against her side.

Someone came by the garage with that thing. It was so old and broken it wasn't worth fixing. Your father bought it on the spot.

Abay set the bucket down and attacked the kitchen floor with the rag end of the mop. Firuzeh danced backwards to avoid the suds.

Where's Atay? Nour said.

He went back to work. Drove that wreck here on his lunch break. A colleague came with him to drive him back.

I've seen worse, Firuzeh offered.

Yeah, in Afghanistan.

Wow, helpful. Do your homework, Nour.

Why don't you do yours?

Don't have any.

Me neither.

How lucky you are, Abay said. In that case, Firuzeh, you can finish this floor. And Nour—

I have maths! he yelped, flinging himself down on the rug.

Grumbling, Firuzeh took the mop and swabbed the kitchen's brown-printed vinyl tiles.

Abay plunged her arms up to her elbows in the dish-filled sink.

Ya Firuzeh, what will we do with this car?

Take it out back and shoot it, Firuzeh said, her voice too low for Abay to hear.

Your father says he needs it for his job, three buses and one-and-a-half hours is too much—

That car is too much, Nour opined from the floor.

He says we can go shopping in it at night, it's safer. But look at that thing. We'll break our necks. We'll lose control and crash into a tree. And how do we find money for repairs?

Wet plates and glasses squeaked in Abay's hands. Dishwater slopped over the sides of the sink. Extending the mop, Firuzeh wiped the floor on either side of her mother's feet.

Am I a magician, to magick money out of thin air?

No, Abay, Nour and Firuzeh chorused.

We can't afford that car. Six hundred dollars and a failing transmission! Am I being unreasonable?

No, Abay.

Not at all, Firuzeh said. Besides, when people see him driving that thing—what will they think?

A pause at the sink, as tiny soap bubbles ascended and popped.

Ai, my daughter is mocking me.

Nour said, Firuzeh mocks everyone.

I don't! He can't drive me to school. My friends would laugh. I'd die, she said.

You won't die, Abay said. This is not Kabul. You will ride in that car and be grateful, or else.

But you just said—

Padarnalat, this is your father we're talking about. Show some respect.

Hang on— Nour said.

It's not fair, Firuzeh said.

Good, you're done with the floor. You can mop the bathroom now, if you're sure you don't have any homework.

I have homework, Firuzeh muttered.

I thought you might.

CHAPTER SIX

Grace Nguyen shut the car door and gazed, perplexed, at the tower of plastic containers in the passenger seat. The names had escaped her—osh something, pillow?—but the rich smells saturated her car. The woman she was tutoring had insisted. She had sized up Grace's beer-and-ramen frame and made a beeline for the fridge, issuing directions as she went. Her kids plied Grace with tea, almonds, and raisins. The husband, Omid, had watched in silence while Bahar Daizangi packed meal after meal. Grace blushed at all the fuss.

She had signed up for the program because it was the right thing to do, no matter how the politicians ranted, and because the experience would look good on her résumé. She had not needed the flyers on the Tampa and SIEV X handed to her by unwashed socialists who showed up after talks; she had thoroughly educated herself. But what she had not expected was immediately becoming the object of her clients' charity.

Mrs Daizangi's cooking would last her a week.

Humming along to the radio, Grace drove through the soft dark of early spring back to her flat. She shared the place with two other students, Hannah and Olivia, and Kylie, an eremitic mol-bio postdoc.

Hannah and Olivia were ensconced on the couch per usual, textbooks on their knees, the TV on. As Grace staggered in with her armful of food and kicked off her boots, two noses rose inquiringly.

"What's that?" Hannah said. "You get Indian?"

"Nah," Olivia said, "she was out giving refugees a fair go."

"Then where's the food from?"

"My students," Grace said, setting the containers down.

As one unit, her roommates abandoned the couch to hover over the kitchen counter.

"Some students," Hannah said. "Sign me up for *that.*"

"Need a hand?" Olivia said.

"I'm all right."

"I mean, maybe they want to poison you. You never know with refugees. I could try a bit, and if I don't die, you know it's safe."

"Olivia."

"Okay, okay, but what if their kitchen is unhygienic? You wouldn't know until you're doubled up and chundering into the loo."

Hannah said, "I'll trade you a sixer of Carlton."

"Done. Grab a plate."

Olivia made puppy eyes at Grace. "What about me?"

"Take over dish duty for the rest of the week?"

"You're a monster, Gracie, really you are. Was yesterday's date that terrible?"

Grace tumbled a forkful of rice rich with sultanas and meat out of its container and into a bowl.

"Oh, fine. I'm on dishes. Now pass that over."

Each of them put a bite of aush or palao in her mouth.

After a while, Hannah said, "I'll sign up as a tutor tomorrow."

"You can't. Our last training sesh finished last week. There won't be another until the spring."

"Who knows," Olivia said. "We might run out of refugees by then."

Grace said: "Or we might find a heart, wake up, and end this Pacific Final Solution—"

"Oh, no. Don't you start."

Hannah said, "What are they like, your students?"

Grace thought. There was plenty she could say. Their address was not in the worst neighbourhood, though the rust bucket out front did them no favours.

There was no table in their flat, only pillows, rugs, and those plush red blankets favoured by aunties of a prior generation.

The children were exquisitely polite, quiet and invisible when they weren't helping out. It boggled the mind. At their age Grace had picked fights at school and come home with split lips, shiners, and the long brown hair of one opponent scrunched up in her fist.

Omid Daizangi had merely nodded when Grace stuck out her hand to him. Bahar had enveloped her in a hug. Your face! she had said. Like my face! You are Afghan? Vietnamese, Grace said, smiling. Here are the books we'll use.

"Normal," Grace said, "but different."

"That's very detailed, Grace."

"I don't know what I'm supposed to say."

"Maybe tutors have confidentiality agreements," Olivia said. "Like counsellors. Like Catholic priests."

Hannah said, "Olivia. Don't be so blonde."

"They live in a pretty ordinary place. No shoes in the house, like civilized people."

"Hmph," said Olivia. "How's their English?"

"It'll get better. My parents didn't know English when they came. Now their daughter can swear the parrot off a sailor's shoulder. That's the Australian Dream, isn't it?"

A door opened elsewhere in the flat. Someone shuffled down the hall.

"I don't believe it," Hannah said. "We're going to have a Kylie sighting."

The bleary-eyed postdoc put her head around the corner. "What is that mysterious, magnificent smell?"

"Grace's students made her takeaway."

Grace said, "Aren't you supposed to be in the lab?"

"It's a twelve-hour experiment. I'll bike in at midnight to turn off the cameras. So: a nap."

"At 8 p.m.?"

"We've all made poor life decisions."

"What are you filming?" Olivia said.

"Zebrafish blastulas."

"I'm sorry I asked."

Grace said, "Come try some of this."

Kylie licked a sauced spoon, then piled up a plate. "Did I hear Hannah say your students cooked this?"

Hannah said, "Some refugees in Dandy. Grace is tutoring EAL."

"Refugees can afford to give away food?"

Grace flushed. "I don't know. It happened so fast. One minute we were talking articles—*a, the*—those don't exist in Persian, did you know?"

"Weird," Olivia said.

"The next thing I know, I have all this food in my hands. And I'm outside and she's saying goodnight. Mrs Daizangi, I mean."

"A likely story," Kylie said.

"You're right, though. I shouldn't be taking from them. This won't happen again."

"Boo," Olivia said.

Hannah said, "But what if they're insistent and forceful and stuff?"

"Then I'll be insistent and forceful back."

"Really," Kylie said, "if you think about it, *we* should be cooking food for *them*."

The four women in the kitchen thought about it.

"Nah," Hannah said.

"No time," Kylie said.

Olivia said, "You all say my cooking's inedible."

"My hands are full with tutoring," Grace said. "Besides, I didn't ask about allergies. Here, Olivia, the washing-up is yours."

"You've exploited a starving uni student. I hope you're proud."

"Prouder than a rooting wallaby."

"Agh," Hannah said. "Some brain bleach, please."

"Hey, I didn't say a wallaby rooting a roo—"

"Now you did. Pass the dish soap, Livvy. Two gulps and I'll be in a better place."

"You mean a blonder place."

"No, that's bleach," Kylie said. "Olivia, give me the detergent, I'll lock it up until Hannah's urges pass . . ."

"Wallabies," Hannah groaned. "You're a wicked woman, Nguyen."

"Excuse me, who tutored refugees today? And whose arse was on the sofa watching Australian Idol?"

"We get it, we get it," Olivia said, slapping Grace's palm. "Here's your halo. Get outta here."

"Wait, you went out with Peter yesterday," Hannah said. "We haven't squeezed you for details yet."

"Ooh, Peter."

"Time to get back to the lab," Kylie said.

"There's still three and a half hours to midnight," Grace said.

"The lab's quiet," Kylie said, casting her eyes upward. "Unlike here."

"Take me with you."

"Oh no you don't," Olivia said. "You're not getting out of this."

Hannah said, "Did he take you to Nando's? Did you walk on St Kilda beach?"

Olivia said, "He has freckles. You into that?"

"Bye!" Kylie called. The door shut. A bicycle bell jingled.

Olivia racked the last of the plastic containers, wiped her wet hands on the front of her jeans, then pulled a drawer open and fished out a torch. She swung the beam across Grace's eyes.

"Is Peter Winkler a charming bloke? Or a wanker? You have thirty seconds."

"Olivia—" Grace closed her eyes against the light.

Hannah said, "Should I tie her up? Is Peter into ropes and things? There's a roll of twine in that drawer, right?"

"Olivia. Hannah. This isn't funny."

"Nah, this is hilarious."

"Put the torch down."

"Geez, Grace."

Hannah said, "Grace. Chill out. Calm down."

"Fuck off, all of you." Grace grabbed the torch, tossed it back into the drawer, and slammed the drawer with enough force to rattle the dishes.

"Sorry—"

"I said fuck off!" She elbowed through them. The door to her room shut with a satisfying crash.

Behind her, she could hear Olivia saying, "What was *that* about?"

Grace took a deep breath and went to her desk. Touched the photos of family: Mum, Dad, their chubby boxer. A galaxy of relatives. Here and there an uncle or aunt who'd gone missing. Taken for questioning, her má told Grace. Tied to a chair. Torches shining in their eyes. Then her má's face emptied, and she wouldn't say anything more.

"Thanks," Grace said to the photos. For taking the boats. For fighting. For lying. For not giving way. For living. For dying. For working thirteen and fourteen-hour days in a milk bar in Footscray before moving to the hills. For the long-distance phone calls and occasional awkward visits, when Grace was suddenly the rich and pampered relative, her skin unmarked, her scars unseen.

Thanks seemed utterly insufficient.

"Xin cảm ơn," she added, but that wasn't right either.

Her family gazed out at her from their red frames. A debt was a debt was a debt unpaid.

She would call her parents in the morning, before class.

Ask again, fruitlessly, about the blanked-out years. When you hit me, what were you afraid of? When you screamed at me, your face red, your mind far away, what did you see? What happened to you, má and ba, in the unspoken time?

What happened to me?

CHAPTER SEVEN

After her first visit, their English tutor had argued Abay down to a single container. As she left their tenth session with a covered bowl of stew, Atay said, his forehead all ravines: Bahar. You can't keep doing this.

But she's so skinny!

And your own children, are they well fed? What about your husband, who works all day?

She's a guest, Omid. And our teacher. Where's your gratitude?

Where's my gratitude? Where's our money, you mean. Lamb is not cheap. Tomatoes in winter—

And soccer fees, Firuzeh said, finishing a problem in long division.

The league's over, Nour said.

She butters you up, that's what she does. Going on and on about the flavour in your kebabs, how—what was the word?— silky your cream sauces are. Shameless. Doesn't she have a mother of her own?

If she does, that woman's not feeding her right. She'll never get married at this rate.

Maybe the Vietnamese like their wives to be thin.

If she likes my cooking, Omid, is that such a problem? Do you know what our children say to me? Can't I have sandwiches instead? Or: Can I have two dollars to buy a meat pie?

That was Nour, Firuzeh said. Leave me out of this.

They don't know what good food is. Grace knows.

I know when she walks out of here, half the meat in the fridge walks out with her.

That was *once*.

If you're so set on having a pet, I'll buy you some birdseed.

I want a pet, Nour said. I want a kangaroo.

Firuzeh said, Did anyone ever ask me if I wanted a brother?

We can keep it in the backyard, but then it might kick down our clothes.

Because the answer is no. But nobody asked.

The sheets, at least. The rest are too high.

Firuzeh said: What are you babbling about, Nour?

The clothes hoist. Do you think a roo could get at it?

I think a roo kicked out your brains.

Listen, Abay said. I open and deal with all the bills—

Firuzeh said: You mean, Ya Firuzeh, come translate this!

Yes, thank you, Firuzeh. You do a good job.

This was true, even if Firuzeh rolled her eyes every time Abay asked. She read the words aloud: *Thirty days overdue. Penalties assessed. Outstanding balance. Thirty-four dollars and fifty-six cents. Fifty-two dollars and twenty cents.*

The disasters were subtle but heaped up like snow. A form

filled out incorrectly or sent with too few stamps. An overdraft. A parking ticket. A rent cheque that strayed into the glove compartment. An overflowing garbage bin and the crows that gathered and croaked for weeks after the rubbish was hauled away.

Abay spent hours on the phone with their landlord, bank, and utilities, stretching her English vocabulary until it snapped, then continuing in Dari, to the discomposure of the other person on the line. As Abay paced and parleyed, winding the phone cord around her finger, Firuzeh waited in an agony of expectation for the inevitable: Firuzeh! Explain for me!

Sometimes, aji maji la taraji, the fee disappeared, the owed sum diminished, an extension was granted or a payment plan arranged, and Abay hung up the phone triumphant. *See?*

See what, Firuzeh would say.

What your Abay can do with nothing at all.

Then why are you so wasteful? Atay said. I work all day. What do you do?

Cook for ungrateful people.

You watch TV.

Clean up the dirt that you track in.

You spend my money.

I watch our children.

You give their food to strangers.

What do you want me to do, Omid?

I want us to survive. That's what I want. Tomorrow we'll start looking for a job for you. These offices downtown, they need to be cleaned. I'll ask around.

You want me to work? Who will watch Firuzeh and Nour?

I will. Those offices are cleaned at night.

By this point, Firuzeh had read a single sentence in her history book at least twenty times. The letters peeled off the page and danced like insects in front of her eyes.

In some ways they were poorer in Australia than in Kabul, even though Atay earned more as assistant mechanic than he ever had owning his own repair shop. Here, money evaporated, or was nibbled and pecked to nothing by impersonal, automatic rules. One day late: a fee. The wrong address: a fee. Here, people were reluctant to wait for payment. In Kabul, no one had very much, but there were neighbours and relations to beg for favours or a handful of rice. There were periodic hawala transfers from Iran.

Omid, I could ask my parents—

During the war, I would have done anything. Anything for bread for you and the children. Never again.

So you took her money and hated her.

I heard the things she said to you. Your cousin in Tehran with steady construction work, don't you wish you had married him instead? While I cried and kissed feet to turn the rifle away. To come home alive. To come home to you.

That's the way mothers are. If I asked—

This is Australia. All your father's tomans, how much are they worth here? Nothing. They're worth spit.

Don't be angry, Nour said. Atay, I can work—

All right, Abay said. I'll go find a job. Now I know what your sweet words and promises are worth. Less than one toman. Less than my spit.

She wrung out a dishcloth and flapped it dry, then strode into the bedroom and shut the door.

Your mother! Atay said, spreading out his hands.

Can we eat now? Firuzeh said.

Nour said, Is Abay not eating dinner?

Yes, you can. No, she's not.

Firuzeh paid strict attention to her plate. The food in her mouth was gravel and dust. The rice was somehow hard and dry, the qorma watery on the tongue. Anger, strong as asafoetida, perfused the food's flavour. Deadened the tongue. Sulphured every molecule of air.

Nour chewed with a similarly suffering expression.

Atay, Nour said, after their plates were empty, aren't *you* going to eat?

Maybe later. I'm not hungry now.

Long after both Firuzeh and Nour were in bed, they could hear Atay's footsteps traversing the length of the flat: all the way to the front door, a pivot, then back. For a minute he stood silent before his own bedroom door. Shifting from foot to foot. Waiting. But that door did not open. So back he went. Back and forth and back and forth, until their eyes shut, and they slept.

Weeks of phone calls and inquiries later, Abay started leaving dinner on the stove before taking a bus to a cluster of office buildings off Princes Highway.

It's not too bad, Abay told Firuzeh, as Firuzeh dabbed Vaseline on her cracked knuckles.

You're bleeding.

My skin is dry. That's all. They have gloves, but the cleaning fluid still gets in. And sometimes I tear holes in them. Anyway, there are other women there, so I'm not alone. Rajani, for example. She's very—very—

An eloquent hesitation.

Firuzeh said, I know someone like that.

At school? I want to hear—but the time—

Atay came in, tossing down his keys.

Bahar, I heard bad news at work—

Tell me later, I'm going to miss my bus.

Atay turned to watch her go, his eyebrows tenting together. Bahar—

We have bills to pay, she said. Goodbye.

The flyscreen slapped shut. Winter leaked into the room. Sighing, Atay closed and locked the door.

Firuzeh. Nour.

Yes, Atay? the two of them said together.

Are you doing your homework?

Yes, Atay.

Good. Do you want a story?

Firuzeh said: No.

Nour said: Yes.

I'm too old for stories, Firuzeh said.

Well, one day among days, the mullah Nasruddin paraded his donkey through the market. He has fleas! he said. And bad breath! And a temper! He snores and kicks! Someone said, How much are you asking for him? Oh no, the mullah said, he's not for sale. I wanted you to see what I have to deal with.

Atay, Nour said, you told us that a week ago. And the week before that.

Did I?

Yes, Firuzeh said. And the week before that.

She shuffled her papers together and went into her room. Spring was breaking, leaf by bud, galahs and crested cockatoos loud in their finery. In the high window of the room, a grey light lingered.

Nasima sat on Firuzeh's bed.

Shove over, Firuzeh said, setting her books down. Oh no. This is wet, you made everything wet—

Firuzeh, aren't you happy to see me?

Things are different, Nasima. I have friends again. We have a home.

I heard you screaming in your dreams, so I walked to you across the sea.

Everyone has nightmares—

Coral cut my feet. Whales swallowed me. But fine, this isn't a nightmare. You don't need me. Nasima gestured at the blank white walls.

You think this story is over. Everyone feasts and goes home. Happily ever after, job, car, and flat.

She unwound a twig of coral from her shining black hair and stuck it in her mouth. It isn't real, Firuzeh. It's a big, pretty dream. A painted balloon in a razor-wire world.

It feels real.

Dreams always do from the inside. Tell me what's real.

This mattress is real. This carpet is real.

Wrong. They're not real. I'm real. Khalil's real. Where's Khalil? Did you forget about Khalil? Do you only remember when you close your eyes?

He was in Baxter. Maybe they let him out.

Yeah, and maybe they gave him a sports car and two baskets of roses.

Mia's real. Shirin's real.

Am I real, Firuzeh?

—

Tell me. Say that I'm real.

No.

Tell me—

The doorknob turned, and Nour came in. He sniffed the air.

Were you crying in here?

Do I look like it?

No, your eyes turn red and fat. But— He patted the blanket where Nasima had been. This is wet. So you must have been crying, even if your eyes don't look like it. I'm sorry Abay and Atay are so mad.

At least they're not angry with me. Or you.

Nour sat down. I hate it. It feels like I'm stuck in bitumen and can't run away. And something's panting and snuffling and waiting to eat me. Firuzeh, do you get bad dreams?

Maybe. I don't always remember. Why?

The sky outside had darkened to ink. Somewhere, Abay polished a toilet, worked the wringer of a mop bucket, vacuumed a floor.

I always have this dream. Someone's hurt, he's calling, he's alone and afraid, but I can't see him . . .

That's awful.

If I run really fast and do all the drills, it tires me out, and then I don't dream. But the next league doesn't start until spring.

Running helps? Firuzeh said, curious.

Yeah, you should run around sometime. Instead of whispering in a corner with all those girls.

You mean Mia and Shirin.

I mean, come play handball with us. I'll beat you. Everyone will laugh.

That's why I can't, Firuzeh said.

CHAPTER EIGHT

It was summer, nearly Christmas, which meant barbecues. The Richmond Refugee Community Centre held theirs in a park. This once, at Sister Margaret's insistence, Abay drove the car while Atay sat in the passenger seat. Bright yellow *L* stickers were pasted to the car's front and back. Despite Atay's complaints, she didn't so much as graze a kerb, although she drove so slowly the cars around them honked.

The air was fragrant with Abay's lamb kebabs, scorched hot dogs, and sausages splitting with oil. Firuzeh and Nour ate kebabs folded in bread, palao, and more kebabs, and drank cola and cordials until they felt sleepy and sick.

But the moment Mo produced a soccer ball, Nour sprang to his feet, gluttony forgotten, and skipped and gambolled after him.

While no one was paying attention, Firuzeh clambered into a tree and lay down on a branch. The leaves shook and shone. The sky was bright. She might have fallen asleep right there, rocked by the wind, but as her eyelids began to flutter, Atay and another man stopped under the tree.

—not renewing TPVs. Have you heard anything?

Ali Reza shrugged, palms up. Stories. Mostly single men. The government saying, Afghanistan's safe. You can go home now. You know, that old lie.

They wouldn't deport a family—

Who knows, except God?

I tried to tell my wife. She wouldn't listen.

How long until your renewal date?

Two years.

Two years! Two years is forever. Anything might happen in that time. Listen, Omid, don't worry about it. Get another plate. Eat and enjoy the day.

Firuzeh cradled her head in her hands and contemplated the breadth and length of forever. A fleece-white cloud blew over the sun, and the whole day dimmed. Brief, passing, soon gone.

CHAPTER NINE

Precisely when life began to feel manageable, even routine, Firuzeh moved to secondary school. Everything was instantly ten times harder. Over the summer, Mia, Shirin, and Gulalai had transformed into otherworldly creatures. They walked differently, blooming into hips; held themselves differently, throwing their shoulders back; spoke of the boys they derided a year ago with sudden gleams of avarice; and laughed high, brittle, glassy laughs.

Firuzeh observed all of this in bafflement. She had missed something critical; some class, rite, or spell.

That one over there, Mia said, pointing. Liam.

Their biology teacher had brought their class to the aquarium, and now the students trickled between the tanks, clutching blank dichotomous keys.

Shirin said: He's not that cute.

You have terrible taste. Firuzeh, what about you?

Liam might as well have been transparent. He stood in

front of a Pacific octopus, whose arms coiled and uncoiled against the glass.

I like the octopus.

Mia said: Oh Firuzeh. What are we going to do with you?

Have you ever worn lipstick? Shirin demanded. Your own, not your mum's.

I bet she hasn't.

Have you?

No.

Shirin said, Mia—

A tragedy. Firuzeh, makeup is the unalienable right of every blotchy teenage girl.

I'm twelve.

Mia said: It's okay. That's not your fault. Point is, you're horribly overdue. Femininely challenged. Educationally delayed.

Can't blame your parents either, Shirin said. They don't know better. Lucky you've got us.

We'll fix this. I mean, would this parrotfish look as good as it does without makeup?

Firuzeh squinted. Yes?

No. It would not. Observe the bold choice of eyeshadow palette. Plus that orange lip gloss. Without those? Psh. Dead.

Dead?

Fish swim in schools, Firuzeh.

Eh—what?

Wear makeup in school, or you don't survive. It's what my older sister says. A law of physics, like gravity.

Shirin said: Get some lippy on her and she'll understand the point of boys.

Mia said: She might, or she might not. But she'll be less embarrassing.

Then that's the plan.

Don't I get a vote?

Don't be ridiculous, Shirin said.

Anemones fluttered their shy, pale locks. The cilia of a jellyfish drifted by.

Seeing her face darkly in the aquarium glass, Firuzeh imagined her lips an anemone red, her eyelids dusted with parrotfish blue. Rich and strange, like Nasima. A seawater change, to a body better suited for the crushing abyss that was secondary school. Mouth like nightmares. Eyes lamped with hunger. She studied herself so closely, she could almost discern the ridges of bone beneath the skin of her face.

Then the bone stood clear. She turned left and saw Shirin's skull. Turned right and saw Mia's. On the ground, a bright toy detonated. All their skin flew off, pulped like newspaper in rain. So much red. Red to daub the mouth with. A pressurized, pulsing, undersea silence.

Then her ears filled with screams.

Earth to Firuzeh. Hello-o-o, are you there?

Firuzeh blinked. The anemones waved.

I said, Mia continued, her voice aggrieved, we'll have you looking like a bombshell in no time flat.

That's right, Shirin said, you space cadet.

I hope you're nearly done, Ms Brown sang. Two more minutes, then it's time to hand in your work.

Shit.

Crap.

The girls plastered their dichotomous keys against the glass of the tank, pencils reeling.

Firuzeh stared at the forest of blanks on her sheet.

8a, a damp voice whispered to her. Sea dragons. 8b, seahorses.

Thanks, Nasima, Firuzeh said.

CHAPTER TEN

Because the proper application of makeup, meaning full battle colours, required time—much more time than the early-morning slick of camouflage designed to avoid teacher detection—it was determined that Firuzeh's remedial education would take place after the last bell in the second-floor girls' toilet. And because there was no point in doing up their faces and not going anywhere, they would head to the cinema and watch a film afterwards. Mia and Shirin shook hands on this arrangement without paying the slightest heed to Firuzeh's objections.

The cinema's in the shopping centre, Shirin said. And it's just us three and Gulalai. No boys. Even your parents should be fine with that.

But if they aren't, Mia said, don't tell them you're going.

Gulalai's coming?

Shirin said, I'll ask her tomorrow. She looks more grown-up these days, doesn't she? I'd kill for those moonstone studs she's wearing.

I don't think she likes me, Firuzeh said.

Does that matter? Mia said.

Let's be real, Firuzeh, you're not exactly the most likeable person.

But we'll fix that, Mia said.

Right. So next Thursday, second-floor girls', after school. Got that? I'll bring everything I've got—Mia, you too.

Mia said: Don't forget money for the movie ticket.

That afternoon, while her teacher attempted to demystify quadratic equations, Firuzeh wrote and directed her own movie script in her head.

```
INT. HOME — DAY
She'd have tidied up more than usual,
the shoes in neat battalions, the
floors swept without asking, the
garbage emptied, her homework done.
                FIRUZEH
  Abay, can I go to the movies with
  my friends from school?
                  ABAY
              (wrinkling brow)
  Who'll be watching you?
                FIRUZEH
  Shirin's parents will be there. You
  met them at our parents' night.
                  ABAY
  The Iranians? They seemed like
  proper people. How are you getting
  home, in that case?
```

```
                    FIRUZEH
Oh,   her   parents   will   drive   us
back.
```

No. She rewrote the line, redid the shot. A car pulling up in front of her house was not in the budget for special effects.

```
                    FIRUZEH
We'll   walk   home   together   in   a
group.
                     ABAY
What is the movie about?
                    FIRUZEH
A   girl   growing   up   and   fitting
in.   There   aren't   even   boys   in
the   movie,   Abay.   Anyway,   I   don't
ask   you   for   much.   Not   like   Nour.
So   this   once,   please,   Abay,   can
I   go?
                     ABAY
Hmph.
ABAY   fusses,   as   a   mother   ought   to,
then   says:
                     ABAY
It   sounds   harmless.   Here's   six
dollars.   You   can   go.
```

Firuzeh rewound her imagination and watched the scene raptly, again and again, until Mr Williams tapped on her desk. She jumped.

Firuzeh, would you show us how to solve for x?

Ehm—

I can, Gulalai said, waving her arm.

When Firuzeh threw her a grateful look, she glared.

Go ahead, Gulalai.

Gulalai took the marker and worked the problem on the board. A moonstone glimmered in each perfect ear.

So x equals 6.

That's correct.

Gloating, Gulalai sat down.

I hope you paid attention that time, Firuzeh. I need your mind here, not in dreamland.

Firuzeh nodded, her face a hot crimson. Okay.

The bell rang. They all rose, stacking notebooks together.

You're stupid as hammers, Gulalai said as they reached the classroom door. I don't know why Mia and Shirin picked you.

Because I have guts and brains, Firuzeh said.

Guts? Brains? As if.

That's what they said.

They'll say anything to get what they want. I've seen your marks. And you flinch when Mr Williams calls on you. But why they want *you*—

Shirin's going to ask you to a movie, Firuzeh said.

What, they're tired of you already?

No, I'm going too.

If this is a trick, I'm not falling for it.

It's not.

Gulalai sniffed. We'll see, queue jumper.

Now that they no longer attended the same school, Nour usually got home before Firuzeh. She had not accounted for this in her strategy. By the time Firuzeh set down her schoolbag, Nour was buzzing around Abay like a wasp after jam, pausing only for bites from a banana.

It's only a couple of dollars, he said. Twenty cents per. Please?

Where would you even get these sweets?

Caramello Koalas. They're in Woolworths, mum. Or any milk bar. It's only fair, Charlie's parents got the team pizza last week.

You let Charlie's parents pay for you?

Her knife smacked through an onion, dripping outrage.

Relax, mum. It's what you do on a team.

Then I will take you off that team. No son of mine—

It's actually the polite thing to do here, mum. Treating everyone when it's your turn.

And why can't you speak Dari?

You'll never learn English if you don't practice. Come on, madaram. Abay jan. Lotfan. A dollar forty cents. We have that, right? We're not so poor that I can't buy seven lollies, are we?

Abay rinsed her hands, scowling, and reached for her purse. She counted out a scatter of coins, the last few of which had to be hunted for in crevices and corners; tidied them into a column; then caught Nour's wrist as he reached for them.

He squirmed.

This once.

Right, mum. He wiggled his fingers.

Do not let anyone pay for you again.

Course not. Thanks, mum.

He scooped the coins up and fled. Abay turned to Firuzeh, shoulders slumping.

Don't tell me you're asking for money, too.

I—

You know how things are. Nour doesn't understand. We barely have enough for rent this month. It's that fucking car.

Firuzeh swallowed. I don't want any money.

Good. I'm glad to have such a good daughter.

Abay resumed her stance at the cutting board. A line of heart-red tomatoes fell bleeding into slices.

I don't know what I'll tell your father about that money when he asks.

Firuzeh sat down, unzipped her schoolbag, and worked on her algebra problems in silence.

I saw that, Nasima said. Nour gets everything. I heard what Gulalai said at school. But you're good, isn't that right? A good daughter.

Nasima was sitting on top of the television, saltwater trailing from her heels in two lines down the glass.

Oh, don't ignore me, Firuzeh. I'm trying to help. You didn't have nightmares last night, did you? That's because of me.

$$x^2 - 7x + 20 = 8$$

Firuzeh concentrated on the formula so intently that her pencil lead furrowed the page and snapped. She pushed the pencil into a sharpener.

No, I didn't have any nightmares last night.

That's good, Abay said as tomatoes crackled in the pan, oblivious to the dead girl atop the TV.

That's because I tore them to pieces with my teeth. Do you know how to fight a nightmare? Do you even know how a nightmare's made?

No.

You put bits of stories together to make a home or a family. Some you're given, and some you make by living. A nightmare is when the ugliest, most ferocious pieces clump together and go hunting for other stories to eat.

Firuzeh said: You can't fight a story.

You can. Break a nightmare into its little bits of story, and, bam, no more nightmare.

So?

You're living in a nightmare. You should take it apart.

You're nuts.

Be nice to me, Firuzeh, or I'll let the nightmares eat you.

She hopped down from the television with a squelch and leaned over Firuzeh's shoulder, dripping onto the page.

Go away.

x equals four and three, Nasima said. I always was excellent at maths.

Atay, Firuzeh said, I need six dollars.

Atay was watching an Afghan channel on TV. The pale light flickered over his face.

You should have asked Abay.

I forgot. She was so busy today.

What do you need the money for?

Poster board. Glue. Scissors. We're doing a group project— a history presentation. Did you know about the Afghan cameleers, Atay? Afghans were here one hundred fifty years ago. Before trains. Before cranes. Or Prime Ministers.

That's interesting. Let me see.

He opened his wallet and shook out three two-dollar coins and a scattering of change.

And I have to stay late at school on Thursday, to prepare—

Tell your Abay tomorrow.

I will, Atay. Thanks.

Thursday after school, the girls' toilet glittered with Shirin's and Mia's mirth. They brushed shimmering colours on their eyelids and brow bones and rose-pink balms onto their chapped lips. Vinyl pouches on the sink bulged with powder cakes, eyeliner, foundation.

Gulalai uncapped a black tube and sleeked her mouth with lipstick in one elegant stroke, then crossed her arms and leaned against the wall.

You're so slow, Gulalai said.

Mia said, Not everyone is as good at this as you.

One of Shirin's eyelids glimmered rich purple, the other deep blue. Here, Firuzeh, she said. Let's do you.

You don't have to—

It's no problem at all. Hold still.

Gulalai said: Mascara, seriously? Firuzeh's going to give you a sty.

Don't be mean, Gulalai. Mia, pass me the blush.

Gold eyeshadow, Shirin?

Nah, darker. Copper and brown. Don't you think?

Hm, yeah.

Gulalai said: You look hideous.

No, don't open your eyes, I've got to—there.

Firuzeh blinked. The face in the mirror was not quite hers, not quite Abay's. There was a touch or a trace or a thought in it of an old photograph of a maternal aunt, who was either dead now, or in Iran. The face in the mirror was sophisticated. Pretty, even though the fluorescent lights were unkind.

Mia said, We're geniuses, Shirin.

I know.

Are we going to hurry up, Gulalai said with a yawn, or are we going to miss the start of the film?

They skipped down the steps. Liam was waiting at the bottom.

Oh hi, Mia said, linking arms with him, her smile as wide as melon slices.

Not too bad, he said. You girls clean up good.

Firuzeh focused on the footpath, counting the freckles of chewing gum. The afternoon light exposed her lie. Each car on the road was a mirrored threat. She prayed for luck. For Nour to have gone straight home from school. For Abay not to be out.

When they reached the anonymous muddle of the shopping centre, she exhaled in relief.

Students chattered over fried chicken, blotting their mouths. Some sucked helium from balloons with giggles and squeaks. A salesgirl sprayed perfume on a slip of paper and held it out to them. Firuzeh rubbed the paper idly between finger and thumb. It smelled of wealth and carelessness.

They walked past whirring plastic planes and wire cages of soccer balls that would have driven Nour wild; past light-up shoes and mannequins in fresh shirts and dresses, fabrics whispering desire; past bubbling infants in polka-dot strollers who sucked on their fingers and knew nothing but want.

At the cinema, they paid for student tickets, then sank into plush, popcorn-scented seats.

Shirin said: I'm happy you could come.

Me too, Firuzeh said, glad for the theatre's gloom.

I bet her parents don't know, Gulalai said. I bet you didn't tell them.

Shut up, Gulalai, Shirin said.

She looks scared.

I said shut up.

Down the row, Mia laced her fingers through Liam's. She sipped the tall cup of cola he had bought through his straw.

Shameless, Gulalai hissed into Firuzeh's ear. And that bossy Shirin! None of them care about you, you know—

Nasima, soaking a seat one row behind them, silver-white in the light from the screen, leaned forward and murmured: You could end this, you know. All you have to do is say—

Do your parents hate you, Gulalai? Did they want you at all? Is that why you're so hateful? Or do you drink poison for breakfast? Snake poison, yum. That reminds me. Like Shirin said: shut up. I wish you'd go back to Afghanistan.

Firuzeh clamped a hand over her mouth.

The three girls stared at her, eyes wide, breaths sucked up into collarbones. Liam, oblivious, continued watching the previews playing on the screen.

That was a funny one, he said. They make better movies every year.

Yes— Mia managed.

A soft shining began in Gulalai's eyes. They filled like moons, then overflowed.

The movie began.

Nasima said: That's all unravelled. Well done.

I didn't mean to—

Oh no. You did. Girl was telling a story of her own. One where you jumped a queue, swam to Australia, killed her aunt, stole her friends—

I didn't, Firuzeh whispered, do any of that.

No, but that's her story. And you sliced it apart. With a fistful of broken glass, I saw. Where did you get that? A dream? It doesn't matter. You cut her kite. She has no story now.

Gulalai sniffed fast and hard, then breathed slow, with the wet noises of somebody stifling sobs. The movie unrolled onscreen, indifferent to its audience. Once upon a time a girl went to a school where no one was kind and no one cared. She kissed people she didn't like and lied to her parents, and eventually she ran away.

Firuzeh tasted sickly sweet guilt on her lips.

Let me see, Shirin said. The movie was over. She and Firuzeh had huddled in the ladies' to sponge their faces with paper towels and mineral oil. Shirin pursed her lips, licked a finger, and rubbed at one corner of Firuzeh's eye. There, she said. All gone.

Gulalai had bolted long before the credits rolled. Mia had departed arm in arm with Liam, giving an airy farewell without looking back.

Firuzeh said: No one will know?

Gulalai's not going to tell. She's completely humiliated. Besides, she deserved it. And Mia won't remember anyone but Liam. Did you see her face? That leaves me. I'm not a gossip, are you?

I meant this, Firuzeh said, her hand circling her face.

Nah. I did a great job putting it on and an even better job taking it off.

Shirin's face crinkled with mischief.

How do you feel? Do you like boys now?

I still prefer fish.

〽〽〽

Firuzeh let herself in quietly, the key slinking pin by pin into the lock. Atay would be glued to the television. Nour would be dawdling over his homework or else emptying the fridge. Abay was at work. As she eased the door open, the hinge groaned, as usual. Tonight the sound was infernally loud.

Firuzeh slipped inside.

Abay sat in the living room. The TV was dark. Atay leaned against it, head bowed. Nour was nowhere to be seen.

Firuzeh, Abay said, her voice so mild that the wall clock's *snick, snick* nearly drowned it out. Where have you been?

At school—working on—we had a project—

As if Firuzeh had not spoken, Abay said: I went shopping today. To buy lamb and rice. To feed you. At the grocery store, I ran into that Iranian madar from parents' night. How is your daughter Firuzeh, she said. My Shirin talks about her all the time. I said, I am grateful my daughter has such a kind friend. That project they are working on after school today, Firuzeh cannot stop talking about.

Atay did not raise his head. A fine, stinging sweat formed on Firuzeh's palms.

And do you know what she says to me? She stares as if I have grown snake heads and says, What project? The girls are going to the cinema! So, Firuzeh, I ask you one last time—

Firuzeh could not meet her mother's gaze.

Tell me where you got the money, Firuzeh. I called and asked. A movie ticket is eight dollars. Did you steal? Or did you—how could you, how could a daughter of mine—let Shirin pay for it?

I gave her six dollars.

Atay ran his finger along the top of the television.

She said she was buying school supplies.

School supplies! Do you know how your Atay and I work the flesh off of our fingers for you? For you to lie, to disobey, to disrespect us, to sneak around, to take the money we need for bills, to squander, to waste—

You do not know the value of life, Atay said, or the worth of what we gave up for you.

And what's this? Abay said. She seized Firuzeh's wrist and sniffed her hand. Perfume. Where did you get perfume? Did you spend money on that, too? And—your eyes. You lined your eyes. Were you with boys? Of course you were with boys. Here's the proof. Here is my nose and here are my eyes. Do you have no care for what people say?

There weren't any boys, Firuzeh said, her lips numb.

But you are a liar, Atay said. So why should we believe you?

A lying, greedy, deceitful child—

Can I go now? Firuzeh said.

Go ahead, straight to hellfire and the pit. May the grave crush you. Did you forget that paradise lies at the feet of mothers? My feet, right here—

Her slipper punctuated the last few words.

Atay added: Abay won't be paid tonight. Because of you.

Abay said: From now on, you come directly home from school. You may not go anywhere else. For any reason. No parties, no sports, no trips with friends—

Okay, Firuzeh said, her stomach knotted. Can I go now.

Your Atay gave up his business for you. Do you know what would have happened to you if we stayed? Do you know?

That's enough, Atay said. She heard us. Go.

Shaking, Firuzeh went into her room. There was a fort on Nour's bed, constructed with both of their pillows and his race car doona. His eyes gleamed at her from its depths.

Done?

All done, she said, sitting down on her bed.

Where were you?

The cinema.

Did you see something good?

I dunno.

Probably not. Girls watch movies about kissing and stuff. Is that the only thing you did? Abay and Atay were very loud.

Firuzeh said: I also caused six frog species to go extinct, bleached a kilometre of the Great Barrier Reef, and triggered an earthquake in New Zealand.

Nour cocked his head. That's all?

Forgot to mention, I also murdered the PM.

Ooh, Firuzeh. That's very bad. Nour stuck one arm out of his fort and waggled his index finger at her. You can't go killing PMs, they'll stick another one in, and then we have to memorize an extra name. No wonder Abay was so upset. When my history marks come back, I'll blame you.

Her lips twitched.

Nour said: If you want to sleep—

I do, she said. Both their heads swivelled toward the door. A battle raged on the other side.

Nour said: I can do my homework in the bathroom.

No worries, Firuzeh said. I can sleep with the lights on. You don't have to go anywhere.

Thanks.

But you've got to give my pillow back.

CHAPTER ELEVEN

Mrs Sing—"Or Mrs Star," she told her Year 6 students when they giggled or howled in disbelief, "it's a homophone in Cantonese"—took up position at the piano.

"A homo what?" came the perennial cry from the back of the classroom, followed by the annual sniggering.

This year's clown was an Afghan boy with floppy hair that fell in his eyes and a smile as sweet as canned peaches on a plate. His family had TPVs, she had heard. He cracked so many jokes, she would never have guessed.

"A homophone," she said to him, "is one word that sounds like another. Which is something you should have learned in English. Since you are in such a good mood today, Nour, would you warm us up? Sing us this scale—"

Her fingers marched across the keys.

The tones lingered, then melted into air. She nodded encouragement at him.

Nour's mouth pinched tight, all laughter gone.

"Nour? If you could please sing for us—the class is waiting—"

She played the scale for him again. He swallowed. Swelled. Spat out one note, and then another, that bore no relationship to the notes she had struck.

He was tone deaf. With hundreds of students, she had not noticed.

"Thank you," she said. "A good effort. Class—?"

She walked them up the scale, step by wavering step. Then back down: mediant, supertonic, tonic. The boy's face remained flushed and furious.

"Today," Mrs Sing said, then hesitated. She was supposed to teach harmony today, but every nerve in her body jangled and rang. Every chord she played would be dissonant.

Instead, she opened the cabinets that contained percussion instruments donated or collected from op shops around town: tambourines, guiros, maracas, cymbals, triangles, djembes, a snare drum and sticks.

"Today we're making music with these."

A stampede, then a whirlwind of hands. A din and a rattling, a clatter and clang. Nour staggered back with a djembe in his arms.

Mrs Sing clapped her hands, and the uproar subsided.

"If you don't have an instrument, you'll clap and stomp." She provided them with a heartbeat rhythm. *Ta ta too. Clap clap stomp.*

"Now djembes," Mrs Sing said, "play this."

"Now, tambourines. Triangles, this."

For a moment, Mrs Sing was as young as her students again. Squatting, she tapped a thimbled thumb on the floorboards of her father's shop. Pit-a-pat. The thimble beat time to the rhythmic ostinato of the sewing machine. Now slow, now fast. Waves of silk washed under the sewing machine's lip and emerged as jackets and butterfly gowns. The scissors, too, had their own scraping beat. Sometimes she sang, but not too loud, so that her father was not distracted. When the scissors slipped or snagged, and whole dollars of fabric fell ruined to the table, he swore and flung spools of thread at her.

She blinked away the memory and stood once more under the classroom's fluorescent lights, between familiar squared walls.

"Now sing something," she said, "or shout, if you like. Listen. *I am. A tea-cher. My name is. Mrs Star.* Now you."

The student she pointed to blanched. "I don't know what to do."

"Say whatever you want."

"Twen-ty. Plus for-ty. Is six-ty. I think."

"Jake, what about you?"

Jake dropped guiro and scraper and cupped his hands over his mouth. *Btse btse btse btse btse btse . . . tch tch tch!*

"Fantastic," she said. "Your turn, Nour. Keep playing— don't stop!"

"My sis-ter. Is af-raid of. Her sha-dow. And friends."

"Ba-con. And fried eggs. And waf-fles. And Mi-lo."

"Aya Kha-nem. Se-ta-reh. Mezle khar-eh. Ya sag."

Stifled titters, here and there.

"Poetic," Mrs Sing said. "Is that something from home?"

"Obviously."

Around the room they went.

"You'll come. A-waltz-ing. Ma-til-da. With me."

"Co-mo. Se lla-ma. Sí. Bo-ni-ta."

"All right," she said. "On my signal, triangles, drop out. Ready . . . now. Okay, tambourines."

She stretched an invisible measuring tape between her hands, again and again, and one at a time the instruments stilled. At last there were only feet and hands. *Clap clap stomp. Clap clap stomp.* She called for the feet to stop, and for a moment there was only the simple living sound of one hand against the other, a thimble bouncing against the floor, a slap—

Then, with a final gesture, she cut that off, too. The room crackled and prickled with the sudden quiet. They all held their breaths. Even Nour. Even Jake.

"Excellent," she said. "Now we'll write down the patterns that we played."

Her marker squeaked against the board. "That was 4/4 time," she said. "Who can tell me what these numbers mean? Megan? Yes. Very good. This is the rhythm we clapped and stomped. Name these notes for me, someone."

"Crochet, crochet, minim."

"Good. Now show me."

They named and counted their way through all the silty layers of rhythm their river had laid down. Then the bell rang. Class was over.

"Nour," Mrs Sing said, "would you stay a minute?"

Jake *oo-oo-oohed*, and Nour flung him a look of scorn.

When the classroom had cleared, he said, "Am I in trouble?"

"No. I wanted to ask your advice. What Juma said—that was Persian, right?"

"Maybe," Nour said, studying his shoes.

"I saw that you laughed."

"It was a dumb joke."

"About me?" She watched him. "He won't get in trouble."

"I'll talk to him," Nour said, not meeting her eyes. Thumbs hooked together, hands straining apart. "I'll tell him not to do that again."

"I would appreciate that."

She nodded at Nour, dismissing him. Cymbal by drum, she collected the instruments her students had left around the room.

Mrs Sing said, half to herself, "That Juma. I must be getting old."

"Not if you're still noticing this stuff," Nour said from the door. A quicksilver smile, and he was gone.

He was a curious boy. So many of them were. There was perhaps no other school in the greater Melbourne area, perhaps no other school in Australia, that had so many children of war. Some shy, some loud, some laughing, some quiet—and every one of them on a hair trigger. Every one of them swallowing barrels and buckets of the wrath, frustration, grief, and shame that other Year 6 students sipped in juice-box amounts.

Mrs Sing was born decades after war swept through Hong Kong. Nevertheless, war had left deep handprints across her life. Her grandfather, gasping himself awake. Her father, scarred with secondhand terror, biting and snapping like a beaten dog. And now her classroom was full of children of a different war.

She had a whole golden hour before her next class. Mrs Sing took her syllabi and curriculum—both of which she would have to revise, rearranging later units of Rhythm and Genre and Period to fit in a unit of Harmony—and walked with whipstitch steps to the teacher's lounge.

"They can't," Mrs Pierce said. "They can't do that."

Mr Early said, "I'm afraid they already have."

"That's Canberra for you."

Ms Anderson said, very quietly, "I'm going to a protest Saturday. If anyone would like to join."

"On the bright side, there'll be more time and resources to go around—for the ones that are left."

"If it's not about educational policy, what the government does is none of our business."

"It affects our students."

"So does the flu."

"If I'm interrupting," Mrs Sing said, "I'd be happy to leave."

"Nah, Shelly, we're talking politics." Mr Early shrugged. "Which, well, we shouldn't be. But it appears that we are."

"It's this TPV business," Mrs Pierce said.

"Did something happen?"

"There's a Year 8 student at the high school, maybe you taught her . . . Anyway. Her family's visa renewals were denied. DIMA took the father into custody. But they'll be deported together, is what I heard."

"Who was it?" Mrs Sing heard herself asking from afar, as if her voice belonged to someone else.

"The name that I heard was Gulalai Zahir."

"I had her in maths," Mr Early said. "Bright girl."

Ms Anderson said, "She always had a brave face on. But I thought there was a deep sadness there."

"She couldn't have known, though."

"The thing about TPVs," Mr Early said, "is that they're inherently destabilizing. Try to get a job with one of those. 'What's your five-year plan for working here?' 'Uh, I can't say, I might be deported in three years.' "

"It's heartless," one of the others said. "Heartless and evil. I'm ashamed of it."

"I don't think our government would do anything evil. Besides, isn't Afghanistan safer these days? With the Americans there, and everything?"

Mr Early said, "I haven't heard much in the news lately."

"That's good. Isn't it?"

"I remember her," Mrs Sing said, a face and voice finally coming to mind. Contralto, a timbre like warm milk and honey.

"Here's a flyer," Ms Anderson said. "The protest is Saturday."

Mrs Sing noted the date and time. "I have a choir concert in the morning."

"Bring the choir."

"You can't be serious." She thought about it. "I might."

Mrs Sing did not revise her syllabi that day. She had four more classes, then a rehearsal for the musical, and by the time she reached home a headache throbbed at the back of her skull: crochet, crochet rest; crochet, crochet rest.

"Hurry up and sit down," her husband said. "Dinner's getting cold. And I'm starving."

She sat, wincing, and they ate in silence.

After clearing half his plate of braised pork, eggplant, and tomatoes in eggs, he pushed back from the table. "Xuelai, what's wrong?"

"Nothing," she said, then grimaced. "A headache."

"Kids acting up again?"

"No." She rubbed her temples. "I mean, they always do. It's just, today—"

"Here." He set a water glass and two tablets on the table.

"This is an awful world," she said. "These kids, my kids, they deal with so much—" She lifted a slice of eggplant to her mouth, paused, then put it back. "Chengming. I want to stop trying."

"They must have been monsters today."

"It's not my current students. A former one. Her name was Gulalai."

Crochet, crochet rest. She clapped the tablets into her mouth and gulped the glass of water.

Her husband stiffened. "You're serious."

"I didn't know until today. I'm sorry."

"If it's the money—"

"As if money could stop a bullet. Or a bayonet."

"Xuelai, we live in Australia."

"That's right," she said. "We live in Australia. I will not have a child here. Do you know what we're willing to do to children?"

"What am I supposed to say? Do you want us to leave?"

"No."

"But you don't want us to stay."

"I don't know."

"You were impossible in college," her husband said. "You're impossible now."

"Having a child takes faith, or optimism. I don't have much of either left. Anyway," she said, "if we're talking about college, you couldn't cook. You called your mother long-distance to ask how to boil eggs—that was two hundred dollars. I should tell your colleagues that sometime."

"There's nothing to it," he said. "It's chemistry."

But beneath his lightness was an injury. She had wounded him, she saw, just as the day had wounded her: thoughtlessly, irreparably, the way a crane dangling a steel girder might gash the beams around it. And she could not tend to that injury while her own was so raw.

"Thanks for cooking," she said. "I'll do the dishes."

Chengming took them anyway. "I hope you'll feel different in the morning," he said.

"I won't."

"Then we'll both have decisions to make."

"I know. Whether we still need all this space. If. And whether I should take my choir kids on an excursion. It's a lot of paperwork."

"Of all the things you could be thinking about . . ."

"Why not? It's the natural thing to do. If I want to be more involved. Ha, listen to me. As if I could have any kind of effect on a machine this big. On a world this cold."

"Xuelai, I don't understand you."

"Maybe not," she said, the headache returning. "And maybe that's for the best."

Crochet, crochet with fermata. Rest.

CHAPTER TWELVE

That Gulalai had vanished from school became Firuzeh's private shame and joy. She did not think to inform either Atay or Abay, who in the best case would worry and in the worst would fight. Now that she was thirteen, and wise, she was aware of their terrible fragility, like a pair of gilt teacups on the edge of a shelf. She was careful not to overfill or unsettle them, although Nour, who had achieved no such enlightenment, kept trying their tempers regularly.

Firuzeh, of course, considered herself wholly responsible for Gulalai's disappearance.

We need stories as much as bread and sleep. I took hers away.

Nasima said: You gave her a chance to tell a better one.

I wrote her out of existence.

You and the federal government.

I was the nightmare.

Nasima allowed that this might have been true.

So preoccupied was Firuzeh with Gulalai's fate that she did not grasp at first the abrupt rearrangement of their lives.

The earliest indication was Atay's ancient car at the kerb on a day when he would normally be at work.

Firuzeh watched him through the kitchen window, where she stood washing dishes left from a guest. She rinsed and dried teacup after rose-painted teacup, and still Atay idled inside his car. Then, by degrees, he bent until his forehead was pressed against the steering wheel.

Abay, Firuzeh said, Atay's home.

Is he?

Something false, like paint, in her mother's voice.

He's sitting outside. Why doesn't he come in?

Maybe he has to take a phone call.

Firuzeh glanced at her father again. I don't think Atay is on his phone.

Then maybe he's afraid of us. Have you done anything to frighten your father lately? No? He looks like a hero preparing to climb Mount Qaf, where the peris and jinn wait to torment him.

Abay. I'm too old for that kind of thing.

Nour said: I'm not too old. Abay, tell me what happens next.

The door opened, and Atay came inside. Cleared his throat. Met Abay's gaze.

Shh, Atay, Abay's in the middle of a story.

They didn't? Abay said.

Atay said: I'm sorry, Bahar.

That's finished, then.

I think we should call Sister Margaret.

Feeling slow and stupid, Firuzeh said, Why?

Because we need her.

Nour said: Atay, why do we need her?

That reminds me, Atay said. Don't you have soccer practice?

That's tomorrow. But Jake and Aaron said they were taking a ball to the park. Abay said I couldn't go.

If you're taking him, Abay said, go ahead.

I'll drive you, Atay said to Nour. Nour beamed and ran for his soccer boots.

Atay went to renew our visas, Firuzeh said, as soon as the door shut and locked behind them. Didn't he.

Who taught you to be so perceptive? You'll only get in trouble, seeing things like that.

It's been three years, Firuzeh said.

You've grown so much, Abay said. I didn't realize. There was always one thing or another. Bills. Rent. Fines.

Abay lifted the phone, punched in a number, and wrapped the coiling cord around finger and thumb.

Did they not renew our visas, Abay?

St Kilda Sanctuary? Hello, is Sister Margaret there?

Abay, why aren't you answering?

Sister Margaret, it's Bahar . . . How are you doing? I am so sorry to bother you, but Omid said I should call. Yes, my Omid. You sound surprised. We have a small problem today. You see, the visa renewals—well. Yes, I am home. No, I've called in sick tonight. Yes, that would be—thank you. See you soon, Sister Margaret. Goodbye.

Abay replaced the phone. She frowned at her fingers, which were snarled in the spiral cord.

What are you standing there for? Abay said. Sister Margaret is coming, and she'll need tea.

Yes, Abay.

Abay said: And don't be crying like that when the sister gets here. She blotted her own eyes with a corner of her scarf. You cry too much, you'll salt the tea.

Shortly thereafter, Firuzeh was dispatched to the Lebanese bakery, where she bought a paper box of pastries dusted with pistachio. The whole way home, she swung it from her finger by its ribbon loop. Currawongs scattered ahead of her. The gum trees were unravelling in strips; the starry leaves of liquidambars flamed scarlet and gold.

Sister Margaret's loafers sat by the door to their flat.

Inside, the sister said: I think they're bluffing. I hope so. Either way, we'll do our best.

We waited, Abay said. We waited so long. And we worked. Look at my hands.

You did everything.

Now this. Abay sighed, twisting her hands together. Then glanced up. Where have you been, janam? Bring those here. And a plate, our mehman doesn't have a plate—

What should we do? Firuzeh said.

We file an appeal, Sister Margaret said.

Will that work? Abay said.

We won't know without trying. Firuzeh, darling, can you write a letter?

What kind of letter?

About your family, and why you came here. What detention was like. If I can, I'll get it to the PM.

The sister put a piece of pastry into her mouth and wiped the honey from her thumb. Her crucifix had acquired a shadow of tarnish, and a moth had nibbled two small holes on the back of her sweater, where she could not see.

Okay, Firuzeh said.

She flopped to the floor with a notebook and pencil. How should she begin?

Dear Honourable Mr President Prime Minister Sir. Please don't send us back to Afghanistan. We left because I wasn't safe.

Tapping the pencil against her nose, she underlined. Bit her lip. Crossed out, scratched through.

Dear motherfucker—

Dear man at the 901 stop—

. . . we have the number of a barrister in Canberra . . .

You said wait. We waited. In Nauru, where they put Abay in jail. Where Khalil. With pills and paper cups. With the rain coming in. There aren't any mirrors in the camp anymore. They took the glass out of every one. Because Khalil. Because Mansour, Mr Nobody, Mr Hassani.

I had a friend. Her name was Zahra.

I had a friend. Her name was Nasima.

It's not fair to you, Sister Margaret said. Not in the least.

Is anything in life fair? Abay said. Or does everything teach us to submit to God?

Perhaps. But even so, we'll fight.

You said stay and Atay laughed, laughed like a war plane, like bombs bursting, and Abay danced. In our new home, on the first night. My mum danced like a girl. And we stayed.

Now you say, time's up, go away, we don't want you.

It's true that my brother can be a real shit.

It's true that I'm not a good or obedient daughter. And my marks once made my mum throw her shoe at me.

But.

Nour burst through the door, mud splattered up to his knees.

Baghlava! he said, delighted, and stretched out his hand. A finger's length from the plate he noticed Abay's skewering glare, then their guest, sipping her tea, trying not to laugh. He backed up and bowed with elaborate courtesy.

Shower, Abay said. Now.

Atay entered, cheeks bright with cold.

I was sorry to hear, Sister Margaret said. But nothing's finished yet.

This is our home. You can't make us go.

CHAPTER THIRTEEN

After Sister Margaret exhausted their legal options, thirty days remained before deportation. The finals of Nour's soccer tournament were forty-two days away. He reminded them at every opportunity.

Abay opened the mail and made two piles: the mint-green rectangles of their plane tickets in one, the bills they would not have to pay in the other.

When I block a goal shot, Atay, like this—you'll cheer for me, won't you?

Of course, janam.

Abay, Firuzeh, you'll be at the finals, won't you? If our team makes it? You have to be.

Abay moved to the sink, rolled back her sleeves, and began scouring a pot with military efficiency. Suds flew, dishwater splashed, and Nour and Firuzeh backed away.

All of us will be in Kabul, Firuzeh said.

We can't go. My team needs me.

Too bad.

Atay said, You can play soccer with your cousins when we're back.

Which cousins? Firuzeh said.

Atay said, Amu Hassan's three boys. We'll stay with your Amu for as long as we need to, until we find a new place. He'll meet us at the airport.

We're staying at Amu's? What happened to our house?

Atay made an unintelligible sound and stabbed a button on the remote.

The clean pot rang against the counter.

It's gone, Abay said. Don't ask any more.

What about the furniture, Firuzeh said, that we left with our neighbours—

That's gone too.

From everything to nothing, Nasima said. Again. What a story, your family's. Over and over, without an end.

Firuzeh said, I don't like how this story is going.

Atay said, That makes two of us.

You can change it, Nasima said. If you want. If you're brave. If you remember how.

Firuzeh said: There must be something we can do. There's always something. The hero has to win.

Atay said, Sometimes the hero dies.

Atay, why are you sitting there? Why aren't you fighting? Why don't you try?

Firuzeh jan, I am very tired.

He's afraid, Abay said without looking at them. Her fingers rubbed grease from their melamine plates. Your Atay has always been afraid.

That's not true, Nour said, sticking out his lip.

Firuzeh said: Atay's a hero. He spears lions and dragons through and through. He'll trick the evil div Dimia. He'll cut off its head.

Enough, Atay said quietly. Your mother is right.

Firuzeh pressed on. She would tell this story the way it should be told.

You'll ride your spotted horse—the car, I mean—up to Dimia's office, and you'll swing the truth at them like a sword. Can't you see how Afghanistan really is? We can't go back; we'll all be killed. And the truth will stab them straight through the heart. You'll take the letter I wrote to the Prime Minister—

Yes, Abay said. About that letter.

—and make him read it. He'll say, I never knew. You're free to stay. Australia needs a hero like yourself.

Firuzeh, the world doesn't work that way.

Abay said, Sister Margaret read your letter to me. It was full of bad language and disrespect. She said she couldn't send the PM something like that. I ripped it up and threw it away. Why did you think you could write like that? What would people think if they saw?

At least I tried, Firuzeh said. That's more than you can say.

With the faintest of smiles, Atay said: I knew we named you well. Hard as stone. Hungry for victory.

So who sneezed and screwed up in naming you?

Nour said: I'm playing in that soccer game. I'll run away if I have to.

Abay said: You're not going anywhere.

I am. You'll say, Where's Nour? and look for me, but it'll be too late.

Firuzeh said: As if we'd even care.

Atay said, Bahar, how are these my children? Is this what you've raised them to be?

I?

Yes, you're their mother, aren't you? Some mother you are!

Who said to his wife, go out and work? Who said, I will watch the children at night? *Your* children! I made them, I kept them safe, even when there was no safety for me! Who let the guards strip his wife naked? Who trusted our lives to faithless men?

Don't push me, Bahar.

You can't keep me from speaking here. Maybe among your brothers you'll be brave again. Brave enough to blame your wives.

I am warning you.

My mother was right. I didn't marry a man. You're nothing but a frightened boy.

The wet pans and plates trembled in sympathy at the flat dead sound of his palm on her face. After that, a lambswool silence fell.

With infinite gentleness, Abay raised a hand to her cheek. Lowered it, just as gently. Went down the hall. The lock on the bedroom door clicked home.

Atay was breathing heavily. He looked at Nour and Firuzeh.

Don't start, he said.

Nour's eyes welled up, but he did not make a sound.

Nasima said: What a nightmare.

Firuzeh said: I hate you, Atay. I wish you were dead.

Padarnalat, I gave you life. I saved us time and time again. You didn't know. You'll never know.

Does any of that even matter now?

What an ungrateful daughter you are. Just like your mother and grandmother. As full of poison as fifty snakes.

Wow, Nasima said. Tell him to jump off a cliff.

Firuzeh said: We're going back to Afghanistan. That's worse than jumping off a cliff.

Atay said: It's happening. Whether or not any of us want it to. There's nothing I can do, dokhtaram. If there was, I'd have done it.

Firuzeh said: I can change our story.

Stupid, Atay said. A big mouth and a brain crazy with dreams. What will that get you, in Kabul? A bullet. He cocked a finger against his head. I should have been much stricter with you. How will you survive, how will any of us—

Firuzeh went into her room. Nour followed her.

In the living room, Atay began to weep.

At school, Firuzeh was already dead. She had not breathed a word of the news, and yet tragedy emanated from her pores. Other students pressed against the wall when she passed. Whole lunch tables emptied when she sat down. Five times a day she ducked into the girls' to search the mirrors for what everyone else saw: drowned, bloated skin, seaweed for hair, the skull stark beneath her cheeks and lips.

All she saw was herself.

But that was not much better.

If she glanced up from her notes, or an exam, she could catch a teacher watching her with a face soft with pity. Do something, she wanted to scream at them. Are you going to sit there and let me disappear?

Ms Jones said: It was a pleasure having you in this class, and I believe I speak for everyone—

I haven't left yet, Firuzeh said, reddening. Her classmates stared.

No, but—chook, you know what I mean.

Ms Jones took out a handkerchief and wiped her glasses, then her nose.

And I want to say, I will never forget what it was like to be your teacher. Give your family my best.

Then she sniffles, Firuzeh told Nour in outrage, and blows her nose! Like it's her lily-white bum that's being deported! What is this, my funeral?

That's what you get for telling, Nour said.

I didn't tell!

Anyway, it doesn't matter. You'll get on a plane and go back to Afghanistan. Absolutely no one will remember you. Or you could run away, like me.

Don't be silly, Nour.

Suit yourself.

I know you. You'd get hungry in minutes. Before you reached the end of the street, you'd turn around to get a bite.

Oh, right, Nour said, springing to his feet. Lunch was hours ago. It's sandwich time.

Leave some of the tomatoes, or Abay will get angry.

He rummaged through the crisper drawer. Abay's always angry.

Still. Doesn't hurt.

For you, maybe. You're sticking with them.

Stop pretending you'll run away. It's not funny. None of this is funny.

You're turning into her, Nour said with his mouth full.

Who?

Abay. Tone of voice and everything.

That's the most idiotic thing I've ever heard.

Nour plopped down beside her, meat and bread in one hand. Is it any dumber than my plan to stay?

Much dumber.

Firuzeh, you've hurt my feelings.

Do you even have feelings left to hurt?

Yes, and you've hurt all three of them. You better make it up to me.

Fine. Once there was a dumbass who was soccer mad—

Firuzeh!

Okay. Once there was a brave little boy—

Little!?

She sighed. If you don't stop interrupting me—

He's at least eleven. That's not little, Firuzeh. Eleven's almost a man.

This boy didn't want to leave his new home, although his whole family was leaving. Although the government wanted him to. He even had a plane ticket with his name misspelled.

Wait.

N-O-O-R. Go see for yourself.

In a bit.

So the boy packed his bags and snuck away from the home that was no longer his home. In the middle of the night, so no one knew. And he hitched his way into the bush. There he made for himself a bow of spotted gum and hunted wombats and kangaroos. But he didn't know how to cook, she added, so he had to eat them fresh and raw.

Oh, yuck!

No one said running away would be fun.

He could make a fire with a glass bottle, Nour said. There's bound to be some trash like that.

Maybe he finds a glass bottle, fine. Maybe he cooks his meat sometimes. Is it really important?

Yes, Nour said.

Nobody knew where the boy had gone. His family shouted his name up until the minute they got on the plane, in case he was nearby and could hear. Do you think he will be okay? they said. Do you think he is hungry, afraid, and alone? We don't know, they said to each other. Only God knows. And God has not been kind to us.

Nour said: But he was fine.

He was. At night, he could see the Milky Way and the stars that made serpents and peacocks and hares. He pitched a shelter of eucalypt bark, and day after day he shot his bow. It was lonely, since he had no one else. And then he heard that his family was dead.

She stopped.

Nasima said, smiling: Now where did that come from?

You, Firuzeh said. That was you.

What are you talking about? Nour said.

Nasima said: Go on. Finish the story, Firuzeh jan.

Nour said: What are you staring at? There's nothing there.

Firuzeh said, faltering, with one hand on her throat: He heard it from the galahs. The galahs are gossips and like to know the news, so they asked the magpies, who learned it from the crows. And when the boy heard, he curled up in the grass and cried, because now he had neither a family nor a home. All that crying brought black snakes out of the rocks.

His bow! Nour said. Where is his bow?

He dropped it when he heard the news. There it sat, just out of reach.

Nasima said: Then the snakes—

Then the snakes bit him on his feet, and the boy shuddered for several hours while the poison crept up to his heart. The stars looked down, and their eyes were cold.

Nour stared at her, mouth open.

I didn't mean it, Firuzeh said. I didn't.

Nasima said, It's realistic. And he had to hear it. Why not from you?

You're the worst, Nour said. He punched a cushion, kicked the doorframe, and slammed outside without his coat.

What was that? Abay said.

I dunno.

He's going to catch a cold.

How is that my problem? Firuzeh said.

CHAPTER FOURTEEN

The writer was American, barely out of uni, and between finding an international SIM and paying tram fares, she appeared to be entirely out of her depth. She was bunking in a hostel with veterinary students and subsisting for the moment on nothing but green apples and sharp cheese.

Sister Margaret had privately decided that nothing was likely to come of this. A few phone calls and emails had raised her expectations, but the clumsy young woman she had picked up by car—a girl, really—vibrated with such nerves and embarrassment that her edges blurred.

"But how did you pee when you were on the boat?" the writer asked the men they were visiting in Maribyrnong. Sister Margaret shut her eyes.

"There was a bucket," one man said. "Or over the side."

"Why did you run?" the writer said.

"We were in danger."

"What is detention like?" the writer said.

They looked at her, their faces grey.

"It is hell," one of them said eventually.

"Like nothing. All day long."

"There is no point."

The writer jotted their words in a notebook, her forehead pinched. Both the notebook and the stamp on her wrist were red. The stamps marked them as visitors to the detention centre, where asylum seekers paced back and forth behind fences. Sister Margaret visited regularly, whenever she could get her hands on names, which were the keys to the buzzing doors of the detention centre. She brought cookies and cassoulets with her. *You're not forgotten,* she told the men. *We know you're here. We know your names.*

"It's time to go," Sister Margaret said. "There's one more visit we have to make."

They were headed to MITA in Broadmeadows, where single boys were kept, Sister Margaret said. She had saved a loaf of banana bread for them.

Her car peeled onto the highway under a low sun.

"You've done this forever," the writer said.

"Not forever. Though it does feel that way."

"How did you start?"

"I had a calling," Sister Margaret said.

"What do you mean?"

"It's like hearing your name on the radio, when you're alone on a cattle station, but someone far away still knows you're there. And has something to tell you, urgently. Something to ask of you. Something you must do."

The writer said, "I don't understand."

"Tell me," Sister Margaret said. "Why are you—an American—writing this book?"

Several cars went by.

"A good question," the writer said finally. "I've asked myself the same thing many times."

"And?"

"I want to say kindness, or righteous anger. That I'm fixing the world. But that wouldn't be true."

A longer silence.

"It won't let me go," the writer said. "Not until it's done. And there's nothing kind or unkind or noble or selfish about it. It simply is."

"Then you already know what it is to be called."

"All I understand is that I don't understand."

Turning into the car park, Sister Margaret said, "Then you're further along than most of us."

At MITA, the writer consulted her notes and peppered the young men with lists of questions. She scribbled so furiously that Sister Margaret, watching, felt her own hand cramp.

"Where is your family? Do you miss them? Can you call?"

"Why did you leave?"

"What was your life like before?"

"What's your life like now?"

"How is living here? Are you treated well?"

"How long have you waited?"

"When do you think they will let you go?"

One boy quietly brought them toast on foam plates and foam cups of water. Nothing in that place was permanent— not the food, not the dinnerware, not the boys themselves. Sister Margaret knew that all too well.

"That is enough for today," she said.

The writer said, "Are we going somewhere else?"

They drove to the church that housed the Richmond

Refugee Community Centre and walked down the steps to the basement.

"This is Mrs Sorisho," Sister Margaret said. "Samuel. Mohammed. And Grace."

"Glad to meet you," the writer said.

"I'm sorry we're late," Sister Margaret said.

"It's all right," Mrs Sorisho said. "Here, take a plate. Sit down and eat."

The writer devoured the bread and chickpeas and soup with the voraciousness of someone who had been trying to live on apples.

"Where are you from?" she said.

"Why did you come here?

"How bad was it?"

Sister Margaret rubbed the back of her neck, wishing for her small room at St Kilda Sanctuary, with its fresh white sheets on the bed and wildflowers in a blue glass bottle. But she saw very little of that neat, clean room. When she wasn't showing a tactless American around, she was meeting with solicitors and placing calls to whichever MPs she thought might listen.

"The government had your phone lines tapped?

"What do you do now?

"Have you seen your son at all? In photos, even?"

"No," Samuel said. "Never. He's two years old. I drive a forklift—I move pallets of fruit. It was very bad. They were always listening."

Mrs Sorisho said, "You're a writer. Good. You will write about this?"

Mohammed said, grinning, "You must mention how smart and handsome I am."

"Because they should know—the Australian government should know—that we are human beings, that their rules hurt us—"

"I'll try," the writer said, swallowing.

There was additional business at the Centre that night: the organization of a fundraiser, along with schedules of detention centre visits and protests. When the writer began covering huge yawns, running one after the other like waves on the sea, Sister Margaret tapped her on the shoulder.

"There's a family you ought to meet, but they're not here tonight. The Daizangis. They have the sweetest kids. How long are you staying?"

"My flight's in the morning."

"Too bad, then. Here, I'll take you back to your hostel."

In the soft blue evening, bright shopfronts and streetlamps flickered past the car windows. The writer stared out, her head turned away. One thumb worried the notebook in her lap.

"I asked the wrong questions, didn't I?"

"If I were you," Sister Margaret said, "I'd have asked about joy."

"Joy?"

"When you have nothing and no reason to hope, when the odds are impossible and not one but two governments stand against you, how do you laugh? How do you see beauty? How do you still show kindness and love?"

"I don't know. I haven't thought about it."

"Anyone can suffer. But joy—that's hard. Ask about joy."

"Next time," the writer said, "I will."

CHAPTER FIFTEEN

Seven days before their scheduled deportation, Firuzeh came home to a puzzle of pots, pans, and containers on the kitchen counter and spread across the dastarkhan.

Eat, Abay said in a voice like cut wire. There's no use waiting.

Abay's eyes were swollen from crying, but this was no longer unusual. Firuzeh picked a careful path between pans to Abay and hugged her tight as she could. As her nose brushed the cloth of Abay's blouse, she smelled a new odour, astringent and dry.

Where's Nour? Firuzeh said.

At soccer practice.

How lucky is that? Otherwise there'd be nothing left. Where did this come from, anyway? Did Sister Margaret tell people we were going to starve?

Just eat, janam. Don't ask questions today.

Firuzeh opened a foil-wrapped bundle of bread and stuck a warm piece in her mouth.

Arnh oo unger?

I'll eat later.

Oo dohn wahn ee oo wayd?

For Atay? No.

Firuzeh lifted covers and sheets of foil and film. She piled her plate with eggplant, chicken, lamb, soups, stews, palao, sabzi, and more soft bread. The sound of her own chewing was loud in her ears. Abay stood by the window, hands crumpled together, looking everywhere and nowhere.

After she had emptied her heaping plate, Firuzeh licked her fingers and said brightly into the silence: Nour will think he's died and gone to heaven.

Her mother's chin jerked up.

Firuzeh studied the labyrinth of pans, then hopped and skipped to the kitchen, plate in hand.

Know how much I love you? I'm going to do homework. Even though there's no point. It's not like marks matter anymore.

Abay picked up a dish towel and began to scrub an invisible stain in the countertop. Over and over. Her lips screwed tight. As if she was trying not to speak.

An hour snailed past. Firuzeh's pencil trekked through great white wastes, trailing grey nouns, verbs, and prepositions, but after a time she succumbed to boredom and began drawing diamonds and checkerboards.

Outside, a car door slammed. Feet smacked the half-cracked pavers leading up to the flat. Then Nour's nose, followed by the rest of him, burst in and swung like a compass needle to his stomach's true north.

A party! he yelped. Mum! When do we eat?

Please, Abay said. Go right ahead.

Fingers quivering above a kofta kebab, Nour froze.

Abay, what did you say?

I said, you can eat whenever you want.

Nour wadded the kebab into his cheek, then stood on tip-toe and reached for Abay's forehead. Firuzeh, I think Abay might be sick. Can you please check her temperature?

Eat, Abay said, taking down a plate. Eat and don't bother me right now.

But I haven't showered! Or washed my hands—

I don't care.

Nour danced from side to side in an agony of indecision. Yes, but Atay cares, and he'll be home soon. I'll shower first. Thanks, mum!

He vanished. They heard the spit of water on tile. Abay returned the plate to the cupboard and resumed an attitude of lifelessness.

It was eight o'clock. Then eight thirty. Nour, clean, his wet hair uncombed, had demolished most of the cooling spread. Now he sprawled on the floor, plump and satisfied. The tick of the clock was sharp and loud.

Nour said: Shouldn't Atay be home by now?

Abay, Firuzeh said, is something wrong?

Nour said: Besides the bit where we're being deported next week.

Abay said, Atay's not coming home.

Where'd he go? Nour said. Did he run away? Did he steal my idea?

Abay kneaded a fistful of skirt in each hand. Yes, Nour, she said at last. He did.

Nour said: Good. Then I'll find him when I run away, too.

The doorbell squalled.

Shirin's mother stood outside with Shirin. The girls stared at each other through the wire mesh.

I heard the news from Rahima, Shirin's mother said, holding up a covered pan. I'm so sorry. I brought halwa. It was fate—what could he do? The car that fell was meant for him. Are you all right? Are the children all right? Are there insurance forms I can take care of for you?

No, no, please come in, Abay managed. We're fine.

They arranged themselves around the halwa. No one reached forward to cut a piece.

It's too tragic, Shirin's mother said. He wasn't old. They should have noticed the wear on the hoist's fluid lines. Ali Reza's cousin is beside himself. As he should be. On top of the visa denials . . . Life has been so cruel to you. Will they postpone your deportations, do you think?

I don't know, Abay said.

Nour said: Abay, what is she talking about?

Now the three of you are alone. How sad it is!

It's okay, Nour said. Atay's brave and smart. He'll do better than I would out in the bush. No snakes will get him. He'll be safe.

Shirin's gaze crawled from Firuzeh to Nour, then from Nour to Firuzeh. Shirin's mother blinked at them.

Have the children been overcome by grief? Your father is dead and was buried today. An accident at work. Bahar, did you—

You're lying, Nour said. You're a liar. Or a mental patient. Abay, what is she doing in our home?

My mum's not a liar, Shirin said.

Shirin's mother said, not unkindly: Don't be so blind. Why do you think all this food is here?

I— Nour turned in a circle on his knees, taking in the mosaic of mismatched pans. No. Atay ran away. You're wrong.

Abay said: Nour. Enough.

Tell her. Tell her she's wrong.

Shirin's mother said: I find that telling children the truth from the start saves me a headache later.

Why won't you tell her she's wrong? Nour shouted.

Where are your manners, Firuzeh? Abay said. Pour Khanem Farrokhzad another cup of tea.

Oh, no thank you, we'll be going now. Shirin?

Yes, maman.

Firuzeh's hands shook. The thermos she held slopped tea over its sides and scalded her fingers.

Abay shut the door behind their guests.

Firuzeh, put that halwa in the fridge.

And the other food?

Same thing. As much of it as you can fit.

Nour said: Why didn't you say anything to her?

Abay sighed, stacked the empty cups and plates, and carried the dishes to the sink.

In their bedroom, when the lights were out, Nour said, Was that girl a friend of yours? Her mother's mean. A kos-e-fil.

Firuzeh said, Nour. Atay is dead.

Don't tell me you believe her.

Why would she lie?

Why would Abay lie?

To protect us, Firuzeh said. Then, after a long moment: That makes you the man of the house now.

Across the room, Nour lay motionless.

A slow, soft breath.

Is it true? That Atay's dead?

Yes.

Fuck.

Nour—

I don't want to talk. I'm going to sleep.

Nasima said: What a pity.

Did you do this? Firuzeh hissed.

Me? Who cursed her own father and told him to die? You got what you wanted.

I didn't want this!

It certainly could have gone better.

Give Atay back to me.

I can't do that. Besides, if you had to choose—Atay or home? Nour's life, Abay's, and yours, or his? I think I know what you would do.

What kind of choice is that?

One you didn't have to make.

Nour said: Firuzeh? Who are you talking to?

Go look, Nasima said, in the garbage bin.

Firuzeh slid the covers back. She padded barefoot down the hall, flicked the switch, and squinted in the harsh white light. Once her eyes adjusted, she dug into the garbage bin, past sauce and scrapings, tea leaves, apple cores, wet tissues. Her fingers closed on an odd black flake: a scrap of burnt paper.

Then another.

Then a third.

The largest of these still showed pale blue ruling and the remnants of a pencilled word. *Love*—

Down the hall, a door opened.

Abay came into the kitchen, covering her eyes.

What in the name of the merciful God—

Firuzeh, up to her wrists in garbage, said: Atay left a note. Didn't he.

What?

Firuzeh found a fourth cinder and placed it with the rest. Please, Abay. I'm old enough. And I know enough.

Janam, you don't know what you are doing.

Abay stooped for the fragments and shredded them further, then plunged her closed fist into the garbage to bury them.

There. Now let's go wash our hands.

The tap ran cold wakefulness over Firuzeh's skin.

Abay. Please tell me. Did he say why?

Because he loved us. Atay wanted to die for us. You must never repeat this to anyone.

Not even Nour?

Nour especially.

Firuzeh dried her hands on a dishcloth, turned, and looked into her brother's eyes. Abay, rinsing eggshell from her arms, did not see.

Nour pulled his blanket tight around him and retreated as soundlessly as he had arrived.

CHAPTER SIXTEEN

Two days later, Nour did not come home.

As far as anyone could figure, between music and maths, he had walked out of the school and into thin air.

Abay called Firuzeh's school and had her sent home.

I've already talked to the police, she said. They're looking. Everyone is looking. And for what? To deport him. It's enough to make anyone give up on God.

Her eyes were pouched, her shoulders caving.

Firuzeh said: Should we look too?

What's the point? So he can be blown up or shot in Kabul? Abay laughed a hard and bitter laugh. The two of you will stick out there like diamonds in coal. You'll die. We'll all die. But maybe Nour has a chance, if he stays—

Did you call Jake's parents?

They said they haven't seen him.

They would say that, though, wouldn't they? If he was hiding there? Firuzeh reached for the phone. What's their number?

Jake's mother said: Like I told your mum earlier, I don't know a thing. But Jake's home now. Let me put him on. Jake!

So, you're the sister, Jake said.

Did Nour tell you anything?

Some rubbish about going bush, and a volcano, and soccer. I thought he was kidding. I'd have stopped him. I swear.

Firuzeh hung up the phone. Abay, I'm going out to look for him.

Do whatever you want.

Can I have five dollars?

If you're running away too, you'll need more than five dollars.

Abay, I won't run away.

Then don't go too far.

Nour was not in any of the parks within walking distance of his school. Firuzeh shouted his name until her voice cracked. There was no reply.

Nasima said: You could walk for hours and never get to all the houses and yards and shops he might be hiding in.

Are you here to gloat?

Odd as it sounds, your story is important to mine.

You're a nightmare, aren't you. That's what's happening. You're jealous and hungry because you're dead and I'm alive, so you're eating me. Story by story, piece by piece. It's because of you that Gulalai is gone, and Atay is dead, and Nour is missing. You and your help. I don't want it. Go away.

Say it three times and I will, Nasima said, her face dark and still. But listen a minute. Have you asked the jinn where your brother went? They can cross the whole world in a thought.

Oh yes, I'll put on my iron shoes and climb Mount Qaf to talk to them . . . Do you think life's a fairy tale?

I'm serious.

Get lost, Nasima.

That's twice. Be careful.

Ha!

If you're too stubborn to ask, I'll do it for you. And for Nour. Once, I had brothers too.

Nasima closed her eyes, as if listening. All right, stupid, she said. Get on the train to South Yarra. Nour's in the botanic gardens. Be quick.

I don't believe you, Firuzeh said.

Believe whatever you like. But your brother's there. And if you don't find him, someone else will. The jinn talk, and now they know there's a lost boy wandering alone in Melbourne. Soon the divs and peris will hear it too. And your mother has told you, hasn't she, of the peris' red claws, and the divs' sharp teeth.

Why would there be jinn, divs, and peris here? The stories are different in Australia.

Stories go where people go, Nasima said. In dreams, in fresh tellings, in memories. Jinn have been here for over a hundred years. They came with the first Afghans, liked the place, and stayed.

Like you came here with me.

I'll follow you anywhere. Unlike Nour. Even back to Afghanistan.

Nasima smiled.

Maybe it's better if the peris take Nour. He'll be safer with them, and you never liked him anyway.

Firuzeh shut her eyes. I can't hear you. You're not real. I'm normal. We're fine. Nour's just throwing a tantrum, and he'll come home soon. Nasima, we were never friends. Living girls, normal girls, don't talk to dead ones. Go away and don't come back.

She took the white pebble from her pocket and hurled it without looking, as hard as she could.

When she opened her eyes, the world was empty. Some kind of light had gone out of it. Firuzeh knew with an aching certainty that it would not return.

Dead leaves cartwheeled along the footpath, their sharp points scratching across the cement.

At the station, Firuzeh bought a concession ticket and waited for the next train.

The car she boarded was full of students. They jousted with pens, elbows, and knees, holding schoolbags as shields, laughing and shoving each other. Firuzeh hated them with a black and overwhelming passion. Not one of them had to worry about deportation, or a missing brother, or a broken mother and the empty space where Atay had been.

She disembarked at South Yarra.

It was a short walk to the southern gate of the botanic gardens. In the wane of the year, the garden slept. Palms and gums striped green lawns with blue shadows. Buds held their breath and waited for spring.

Signs pointed her toward a volcano, which proved to be a sad concrete cistern clad in tarpaulins and blocked off by temporary fences. Succulents slept on its slopes.

No Nour.

She turned toward the lake. Green ducks approached her, cutting through a thick mat of duckweed. On the far side, a black swan billed the water for crumbs. Firuzeh shouted her brother's name. The ducks changed course.

Nour was not there either.

Invisible bellbirds rang silver notes through the trees. Little white dogs trotted down the path, pulling women in joggers and blazers behind them.

The Yarra gleamed at her like crushed glass.

Firuzeh left the garden and followed the river. Young couples snuggled against each other, making moues and taking photographs. Elderly couples tapped and swung their canes.

High up on a plinth, Queen Victoria glared down with an expression resembling Gulalai's. Someone had markered black moustaches on the surrounding marble nymphs.

Nour, Firuzeh called, her voice reduced to balled-up paper. Nour, it's me. Nour, where are you?

Here.

Nour sat under a bronze statue, hugging his knees. His face was dirty, his eyes red.

What are you doing?

Running away, dummy. I told you, didn't I?

Everybody's looking for you.

But nobody cares. Not really. If you cared, you would have found me ages ago.

I'm not as smart or fast as you think I am.

Is Abay out looking?

Firuzeh did not answer.

Yeah. I didn't think so.

She—Nour, it's only been two days.

Abay lied to us. Everyone lies to us.

Yes.

It's not fair. None of this is fair.

It's not.

So are you here to drag me home?

Not if you don't want me to.

Firuzeh sat down next to him.

Nour said: Are you running away too?

No.

Then why are you here?

Firuzeh patted the statue's cold bronze nose. It was an odd creature, covered in curls, here bluish in colour, here golden, here green.

I came to listen.

Listen?

Tell me a story. Whatever you want.

Nour stared at his feet.

I don't know how to start.

Once there was and once there wasn't—

I'm not stupid. I want to tell it in English. Once upon a time. Then what?

There was.

A boy. A regular, normal boy. He wasn't bad, and he wasn't good. His dad yelled sometimes. His mum cried and lied. His sister was mean. He had friends, but they all went away. Bad things happened to some of them. He dreamed about it, he dreamed he could see them, their mouths stitched up, or their fingers falling piece by piece in the street where a bomb went off. Bad things happened to the boy too, but they were in the past, so he could forget. Until he went to sleep. Then the dreams—

He shivered.

When he was angry, he could not stop being angry. Not for a long, long, very long time.

Except when he ran. The running helped. And people liked it when he blocked a pass or scored a goal. People liked *him*. One boy kissed him, even. Then he didn't dream. Then things were okay.

Then his home decided to spit him out. Him and his family. His dad, who was broken, decided to die. As if all the bad things had been waiting and watching, this whole time. Now they came for him.

So the boy did the only thing he could do.

Nour fell quiet.

What does the boy do after that?

I haven't decided yet. But— He gave her a tiny glare. No snakes.

Telling stories is difficult. Even when you know how they should end. And living's harder.

Are you sure you don't want to run away with me?

Firuzeh said, I can't let Abay get on the plane alone. She needs me, Nour. She needs you too. Even if she doesn't know it. Even if she never says it.

He rolled this idea across his tongue, tilted his head, and scrunched his eyes. At last he nodded.

Firuzeh said: Did you figure out a good ending?

Yes, he said, and took her hand.

The bronze creature smiled down at them.

What is this thing, anyway? Firuzeh said as they stood, brushing grass and leaf mould off their clothes.

Says *jinni* on the plate. It looked nice, so I sat down here.

Firuzeh blinked.

Thank you for taking care of him, she said to the statue. Please tell Nasima I'm sorry.

Nasima? The girl from the boat, who died?

Firuzeh said: She sent the jinni to look for you. A jinni flies faster than thought, you know. Now let's go home.

CHAPTER SEVENTEEN

Sister Margaret called with the news. The deportation order had been deferred for six months.

For humanitarian reasons, she said. That's the official line. But politically it looks terrible to insist on immediate removal after a tragedy like this. The journalists would have a field day. And everyone knows it.

Into that sudden slackening of time rushed bills that once more required payment, phone calls to plead for leniency, insurance forms, profuse apologizes from Ali Reza's cousin, condolences, notices, soccer practices, and schoolwork. None of them could spare a moment to fully feel, much less a breath to mourn.

Abay drove them to Nour's team's final match in Atay's rusted, stuttering car. When they reached the sportsground, Nour bolted from the car. Firuzeh and Abay ascended the grandstand as Nour joined his teammates at the centre of the pitch. Other families fished colas and cordials out of blue eskies.

Though Nour did his best, leaping and diving to block,

three balls slipped past him and plunked into the net. He was sent to the bench, and Aaron took his place at the goal. Abay stood and waved.

A blonde girl glanced at her and laughed.

Blushing, Firuzeh grabbed Abay's elbow and dragged her back down.

Janam, why should I sit? I'm saying hello.

It's embarrassing, mum.

What, waving is now embarrassing? He didn't know where we were sitting.

If I'm wrong, why's Nour ignoring us?

Yes, that's silly. He should be waving back.

Nour spent the rest of the game on the bench while Aaron, enthusiastic, cow-footed Aaron, tripped and missed and lost the ball. With every mistake, Nour's shoulders drooped lower. At last a whistle blew; the game was over. Nour's team had lost, one to thirty-two.

Mustering a smile, Nour said: The team's going to Macca's, mum. Can I—

We don't have the money, Abay said.

Jake says he'll shout me, and his parents will drive—

For the last time, Nour, no.

Abay reached for his hand. Nour jerked away.

You don't want any of us to have fun, he said, so loudly that heads around them swivelled. It's always: what will people think? Well, do you know what people think of you? They're thinking, what an awful mother. They're thinking, what a miserable kid.

Nour, Abay gritted through her teeth.

I should have kept running. I should never have come home.

Then stay here! Abay snapped.

She stormed toward the car park. Firuzeh followed, glancing back at her brother every five or six steps.

Come on, she said. Nour!

I'm not going.

Then Jake was standing beside him, an arm around his shoulders.

You're joining us at Macca's, right?

Yeah, Nour said, his eyes on Firuzeh. If you give me a ride.

That boy! Abay said, slamming into the car. Just like his father! Feckless, careless, irresponsible—

Atay was scared. Maybe Nour's also—

Don't you talk like that about your father!

But you—

Hands fixed vice-like on the wheel, Abay braked and accelerated, braked and accelerated, jolting Firuzeh into silence. Firuzeh cranked down the window and stuck her nose out into the blessedly cool air.

Did I ever tell you the rest of that story? About Khastehkhomar?

Mum, you don't have to—

Well, the woodcutter's wife and Bibinegar burn Khastehkhomar's snakeskin, so he can't change back into a snake. And Khastehkhomar says to Bibinegar, Farewell. If you hadn't burned my skin, we could have been happy for ages—as if! What woman likes to be married to a snake, even one who turns into a man at night? He says, Now I must return to Mount Qaf, where my relatives the peris live. Will I never see you again, his wife says, you whom I love beyond life? He says, only if you walk until you wear out seven pairs of iron shoes. And he vanishes. And she, the idiot, puts on iron shoes and walks for a year and a day.

At the end of the year, she asks whose fields these are that she walks through, and everywhere the answer is the same. They are Khastehkhomar's bride price for Bibinegar. And these donkeys? Same thing. And these wells? Those too. That's how Bibinegar knows she is near Mount Qaf.

She sends her ring to Khastehkhomar through his servant, so he knows his wife is near. And he shows up embarrassed. O Bibinegar, I am engaged to a demoness. But how about you work as a maid until I figure out what to do with you? So she does. She cooks, she cleans, and she outwits the peris, his mother and aunt, who would like nothing better than to eat her whole. At last the wedding day arrives. The peris decide to use her fingers for candles. O Khastehkhomar, she says, what do I do? We'll wrap your fingers in cotton, he says. And they do.

For the wedding procession, Khastehkhomar and the demoness walk thrice times three around the room, and Bibinegar walks ahead of them, her fingers burning to give them light. Khastehkhomar, she cries, my fingers are burning! Bibinegar, he replies, my heart is burning! Which isn't the same thing at all, you know. Then bride and groom retire to bed, and Bibinegar lies down outside their door, crying bitter tears. For love!

In the middle of the night, brave Khastehkhomar kills his demon bride. They flee the peris and are restored as husband and wife. But what kind of life is that? When you know your husband can't protect you, and your feet are worn through, and your fingers are gone.

Firuzeh said nothing. Abay wedged the car against the kerb. They went into the flat.

What a coward Khastehkhomar was, Abay said. Then she crumpled to the carpet and rocked with sobs.

Omid, she keened. Omid, come back, I'll kill you, jigaram, my husband—you selfish ass!

Firuzeh fetched tissues and blotted at her mother's locked eyes and sticky nose and stretched-open mouth, from which terrible sounds came.

It's okay, mum, she said. Hush. Shh.

Tissue after tissue piled up into mountains before Abay's sobs stiffened and slowed.

Firuzeh said: Come on. Let's get you to bed.

She tried to lift Abay's damp, heavy head. Her mother's hair trickled over Firuzeh's wrists, white strands salting the black.

No.

You can't lie here like this. You'll feel better in bed. Maybe you'll fall asleep. I'll make tea. I'll make dinner. Let's go, Abay.

She talked and petted her mother to her feet. Step by swaying step, Abay slumped down the hall, then stood and stared at the bedroom door until Firuzeh opened it.

While Abay sat on the bed, making the short moans of a wounded dove, Firuzeh worked a plastic comb through Abay's sweat-thick hair. Then she lifted her mother's shirt, undid her creaking bra, and pulled her nightgown over her head and down around her softening breasts.

There, Firuzeh said, doesn't that feel better? Now why don't you lie down and rest?

And Abay, unresisting, obeyed.

Firuzeh had a good, quiet cry of her own, then cracked four eggs into a pan. Right as they began to smoke, Nour edged the door ajar, threw her a sideways glance, and said, Is Abay home?

She's asleep.

The door opened wider, and Nour came in.

Some game, she said.

Yeah. I know.

You couldn't have kept your dumb mouth shut?

Please, Nour said. You're just as bad. And Abay needed to yell a bit. She hasn't cried once since—

Good news, Firuzeh said. She cried and cried.

Ah. Sorry. He twirled a pinkie in one ear. For leaving you to deal with that.

You mean lighting the fuse and running away.

I did, didn't I. He sighed. Was it bad?

I've never seen her like that.

And you remember the war.

Some of it, sometimes. Anyway. Here's dinner.

I had Macca's, I'm not starving. What's this? Did you cook?

What else was I supposed to do?

Right, right.

How was Macca's?

Everyone sitting around with big glum faces, eating chips. Hey, I said, at least I wasn't deported! No one laughed. I thought it was a good joke.

That's a terrible joke.

You try cheering up a losing team. Even cheeseburgers didn't work.

I thought I smelled that on your breath. Cheese and pickles and onion.

I'll go brush my teeth. You sure Abay's asleep?

Even if she's awake, I don't think you'll get the ripping-apart you deserve.

What a shame. Without firm discipline, I'll run amok. And then—

What will people think? they said together.

Firuzeh smiled.

If I thought that was happening, I'd smack you myself.

I know you would. He paused. Atay knew when to clap. He was proud of me. After I started playing sevens, he came to pick me up and saw me score a goal. He picked me up, put me on his shoulders, called me Rostam, and said he was my Rakhsh. It's different with Abay. She doesn't know.

She'll figure it out.

Or she'll pull me out of the league.

Or that.

I don't know what I'd do. If I couldn't. If Abay.

Let's worry about that tomorrow, okay? It's late. Let's sleep. But shower first, you smell like pickles and sweat.

I love you too, jigaram, Nour said, rolling his eyes. Hey! Stop that! Ow!

Shower, Firuzeh said, pointing. Now.

CHAPTER EIGHTEEN

I should tell you about my friend, Firuzeh said.

Whatever you want, Shirin said, her eyes moving left and right. School had let out barely minutes before, the first arterial bleed of students already washed away.

Her name was Nasima. We were in a boat with her family. They were going to live with her brothers in Perth.

Yeah, yeah. Same old thing.

Then she died.

What?

A big storm hit us. We were crying, praying. The boat nearly sank. When the waves stopped throwing us around, she was gone.

Shit, Firuzeh. Warn a girl, would you? That's heavy stuff.

Shirin quit bouncing on the balls of her feet and looked straight at Firuzeh.

She really drowned?

Yes. But we promised each other before the storm that we'd stay friends no matter what. So she came back.

Your fucking dead friend came back.

Because she cared, in her own way. She ate nightmares for me. She kissed me to sleep. She said you weren't real, that none of this was, that I was caught in another nightmare and couldn't see. But whenever I wanted, I could take everything apart. I didn't believe her. In the end I told her to go away. And she did.

Good. Otherwise I'd tell you to see a shrink.

I wanted to tell you. Because Gulalai—I think she had someone like that.

Yeah, she had dodgy wiring in the attic. Like you.

We were probably similar in other ways. I wish I'd been kinder.

I don't.

And that's the thing. Gulalai was right.

Firuzeh smiled and walked away.

Hey, wait! Shirin ran after her. Right about what?

About you.

And Firuzeh, now friendless, took the long way home.

In May, as Abay showed signs of stirring from her despondence, the federal government announced the end of TPVs. They would be given permanent protection, Sister Margaret said.

Abay said nothing. She hung up the phone, then took it off its cradle and flung it across the room. When the spiralling wire reached its limit, the handset bounced once and slid, spinning, back toward her.

Then she closed all the curtains and went to bed. It was a long time before she got up again.

By late November, Firuzeh was combing Abay's neglected hair, wrapping and pinning her scarf, and reminding Abay to brush her teeth before she left for a few hours' work at a nearby Macca's.

The job was enough for the rent and food, with some help. Samuel and Mo often came around to fix whatever needed fixing and drop off bags of onions, tomatoes, eggs, and rice. The English tutor, Grace, brought string bags of oranges with every visit. She showed up even when her program no longer required it, even when Abay sat sightless and speechless, leaking tears. Those times, Grace put a pencil in Abay's hand, wrapped her own hand around Abay's, and traced the words she was meant to learn that day.

I'll be able to work soon, Firuzeh said. Then you won't have to worry so much.

Abay, gazing at the wall, said: —

Do you want to go see Atay this weekend?

He was buried in a simple grave in Bunurong, south of town.

—, Abay said.

Nour said, But we went last weekend!

It makes her feel better. It gets her to talk.

Nour said, If we tried, we could get her outside. Right now, before the sun goes down. I saw something this afternoon that I think she will like.

Did you hear that, Abay?

The blank stare swept over her.

I've got her left arm, Firuzeh said.

Ready, Nour said, and grunted. Up!

Although she had wept and slept away most of her flesh, Abay's bones were still heavy, and the two of them struggled to raise her up. But once she stood, compliant and dull, it was not hard to steer her toward the door, to slip shoes onto her cracked feet, and draw her outside.

Where are we going?

Nour said: Anywhere. They're all over the place. But let's go left.

Down the street and around the corner they went, towing Abay behind them. The air was warm and rich with the smells of growing things. Abay shuffled along, head lowered, eyes down, like a widow of war.

Another block, and there they were.

Nour said: Jake told me they're jacarandas. Give them two days and they'll squish brown and smell like garbage, but today . . .

Today the trees bloomed in gentle profusion, soft with slipper flowers the colour of evening clouds. A thick odour like honey left Firuzeh dizzy.

Abay stopped beneath one and gazed up through the twisting branches. They let go of her arms. She put one hand on the scaly bark.

How pretty, Abay said. They should have viewing parties. We used to go to Istalif in the spring, to see the red-purple arghawan. You've probably forgotten. You were very young.

Firuzeh said, I remember.

Nour said, I don't.

Omid would have liked this. He had a weakness for beauty. That's how someone like him wound up with me. But these trees must have been here for years. Why didn't we see?

You were always busy, Firuzeh said. And worried. And scared.

Even if I was. I should have seen.

Nour said, Well, they're not going away. We'll see them to-morrow, and the day after that. And next year, and the year after that.

If God wills. If everything—

Firuzeh said: We can worry about all of that tomorrow. Or the day after, that's even better.

Now how did this daughter of mine grow so wise?

From Atay and you. From stories. From friends.

I'm wise too, aren't I? Nour said.

Firuzeh said, You do ask a lot of whys.

Not funny.

But Abay's smiling.

All right. That joke was okay.

Let's hear you tell a better one.

He thought. I've got a joke about a kangaroo. It's a real kicker, see—

Firuzeh threw a flower at him. They ran from tree to tree, all the way down the street, flinging sticky blue flowers at each other and laughing. The sky purpled and dimmed. When they reached their flat, all of them covered in flowers, Abay un-locked the door, turned on the porch light, and brushed each of them clean before letting them in. And then they were home.

CHAPTER NINETEEN

Firuzeh dreamed.

In this dream was Atay on a yellow horse with rose-petal
spots. He said to her

How you've grown.
And she said
I miss you why did you go away
And he said
Sometimes the hero has to be brave
and leave his family for their own good

And she ran to him, and he climbed down from his horse,
and he smelled like halwa and esfand and Atay

Nasima was there, with pearls as big as cherries in her hair
and coral and kelp around her arms

She said
      Bitch don't say you've forgotten me
Firuzeh said
   How could I? But how are you here?
      O, well, the walls between worlds
      are thin tonight
   Will I see you again?
      You abandoned me, and I've walked on
        as I should have done
         I didn't know
           thank you

And Firuzeh said   He said
   Atay will you—   Of course
   Love her like a daughter—

Come with me Atay said to Nasima we are going the same
direction I believe

   And Nasima will you promise to—

      Give him hell like a proper daughter should?

   That's not what I meant

He won't be alone she said I promise but I can't promise he
won't miss you

That's all right
Be good
both
of you

Goodbye
she said

Firuzeh awoke with seawater drying on her face.

And they stayed on that side of the water,
and we on this.

ACKNOWLEDGMENTS

This book would not exist without Sister Brigid Arthur, who gave generously of her time while I was conducting research in Melbourne. I am also indebted to Pamela Curr, Sophie Peer, Dr. Cynthia Hunter, Javed Nawrozi, and the refugees and asylum seekers in Melbourne and Kabul who were willing to speak with me.

I am grateful to Kevin Sieff for his hospitality in Kabul, Naiem Naiemullah for his invaluable assistance, and to Hayatullah Rahmatzai of the UNHCR in Afghanistan for his time and knowledge.

Markus Hoffman believed in this book even when I'd given up. Liz Gorinsky gave it a home and a name. Martin Cahill gave it wings.

Dr. Eva Hornung provided advice and insight that changed the course of this novel.

The Artist Trust LaSalle Storyteller Award bought me the months I needed to make final revisions.

Jane Zou educated me on Australian school systems. Alex Bertolotto provided auto repair expertise.

Earlier drafts passed through the hands of Allison Green, Alma Garcia de Lilla, Donna Miscolta, Elizabeth Hand, Jennifer D. Munro, Liz Argall, Margo Lanagan, Neil Gaiman, Nicole Idar, Novera A. King, Usman T. Malik, and Vince Haig. The book is better, and I am wiser, for their input.

This book also benefited from collections at the State Library Victoria, the Immigration Discovery Centre, and Cornell and Princeton University Libraries. My deep thanks to the staff and librarians who endured my abuse of interlibrary loans.

Nine years have passed since I started this book, and I have undoubtedly misplaced and omitted names, which I regret. My gratitude is no less for that.

All glory is God's. The errors are mine.